"THE INTELLIGENCE"

a state of equanimity

Pat Grayson

Heart Space Publications
PO Box 1085
Daylesford, Victoria, 3460, Australia
Tel +61 450260348

www.heartspacebooks.com
pat@heartspacebooks.com

Whilst every care has been taken to check the accuracy of the information in this book, the publisher cannot be held responsible for any errors, omissions or originality.

ISBN 978-0-9874997-4-5

Published June 2020 in Melbourne, Australia

F O R E W O R D

I first met Pat three years ago at Rocklyn Yoga Ashram, where I lived as a resident whilst studying and practicing yoga and was given the Sanskrit name *Kripadhara*, which translates as "flow of grace". We have become good friends.

Pat has passionately written *"The Intelligence", a state of equanimity* as a story that nonetheless shows us the way to happiness – a state of equanimity that exists beyond the ego. Based on fictitious characters the journey weaves the ancient teachings of three cultures – Australian Aborigines, Native Americans, and Kalahari Bushmen of Africa – who happily and peacefully inhabited the land with respect and love for all surroundings, mankind and creatures, without onus of ownership.

The unique journey unravels, by leading the reader to question the blockages that prevent people from experiencing Happiness, including: fear, greed, jealousy, ego, and bad habits, all of which can lead to depression and dis-ease. We are challenged to question who we really are, the reason to be, the deep meaning of love, our real needs rather than what we believe we want, respect for our ancestors and their teachings, the attitude of gratitude, communication skills, and sacred respect for life of all beings and nature.

This journey highlights important aspects of spirituality, and how they can impact the status quo in current world conditions, where materialism and social media are mindlessly worshipped and block the manifestation of happiness, resulting in the lack of a balanced lifestyle and the onset of disharmony – discontent and pain in the body, mind, and soul. Without inculcating discipline, respect, and interdependence in life, the busy-ness of everyday living weakens the spiritual connection and foundation. Only with peace of mind can freedom be experienced, and this can be mastered by awareness and creating personal space in which to appreciate the changing seasons of nature and its beauty, and an abundance of life's needs.

Synchronicity has provided divine timing for Pat's message to be released to show how we can remain naturally grounded, being mindful of our spiritual core, in a world that is rife with pain and imbalance. Ancient teachings all focus on a family lifestyle that provides structure and stability – where communication and understanding can be nurtured and lead to trust, respect, and harmony. Much confusion exists out there in today's world, and we need to realize our true purpose in life, and bond together to survive, and create a better way of living for the future.

It is timely to embrace Pat's sharing of wisdom, and powerful life-changing lessons, to inspire you and manifest happiness in your life, which can vibrate, and will be felt by all those with whom you meet – wherever you are. He has managed to challenge our understanding of *Happiness* in a story that touches the deep emotions, and reaches the higher states of consciousness. This book is a spiritual milestone.

Kathy (Kripadhara) Burgum,
author of Celebrate Your Gold Within.

T E S T I M O N I E S

I would just like to say that it was an amazingly powerful read. I have already found myself mulling over many of the concepts presented within the book and expect that I will continue to do so for some time. In short, I thoroughly enjoyed it and was stimulated by both the story and the information that it portrayed. In fact, I can go as far as to report shedding more than just a few tears as the story came to its final pages and Stevie concluded his journey.

Seth falconer, author, All is One (ISBN: 990-205-78098-6 9)

I've just finished reading your manuscript. Before I make any comments, let me just say "congratulations"! I am blown away by the awesome spiritual teachings contained within. They resonated so profoundly with me that I have no doubt whatsoever that this manuscript has largely been channeled. At times, the beauty of the spiritual wisdom almost brought me to tears. You need to do whatever it takes to get this book published and out there to reach as many people as possible. I believe that it not only has the potential to change people's lives but could in essence, save some too. If, for e.g., someone in a similar state of self-destruction like the character Stevie, read this book, think of the positive implications that could spring from it, hence, why I say that it could potentially save lives.

I would like to thank you for sharing such beautiful spiritual wisdom.

Sue Formanowicz (Manager of Book Club, Johannesburg)

The concepts and lessons taught are very powerful. Although I have a sense of most of the lessons, the way you have written them and explained them is excellent – simple enough for new "travelers", but also great reminders for old travelers – and some great new wisdom coming through – almost a higher way of expressing the info as if it's all been taken to another level. It's not just a higher level of your writing, but a higher level for humanity to work with. Like we're now ready for more.

Lynette Rink, creator Little Lion love cards, and Lessons in Love.

I absolutely love the way you've created the story and I think it's awesome and will be beneficial to everybody, no matter what their situation, whether happy or sad. The central message is so strong and powerful and brings one back to center.

Lee (teacher)

I N T R O D U C T I O N

Whilst researching this story, and specifically the Aboriginal component, I learnt that a story finds a teller and it will not rest until the story is told. This story agitated until it was told.

The story is fictitious, as are the characters. Yet the characters are real in the sense that they represent our strengths and weaknesses, fears and insecurities. The messages are also real and will support all who listen to them.

The character Weishka is real, as the back pages reflect. Yet, he was an entity.

When I was chosen to tell this story, it changed my life, as I was not allowed to write it without living the concepts – I have had to live the lessons I wrote about. This has not been easy, but is has been worth it.

Workbook as well as a novel;

This is a work of fiction, it is also a workbook. The book contains many concepts. Concepts that are likely to affect you. As they do, record them in the space at the back of the book.

Pat Grayson 2019

Rob Filmer
2-8-1964 to 10-11-2010

I had known Rob for some two years before his passing. By the time we met the diabetes had engulfed him by taking his sight and ravaging his body. For most of that time he was in a bad way, with every other week being rushed to emergency. Finally, the angels reached out for him – his work here finished.

I remember our conversations, pretty much one-sided, where, with the greatest humility he would enquire about my world. As I told him of my latest book or writings, he would listen as if my words were the most important he was to hear. He was like this with everyone.

All of my visits were pleasant, even with the background hum, blinking lights and occasional beep of the dialysis machine. Periodically Julie, would come in and make an adjustment to the machine. She would smile, and fondly touch Rob before heading back to the feast preparation, amidst the laughter and conversations with the many loved-ones that always filled the house.

When Rob did talk, it was usually of an uplifting episode from his life. There were lots of these and all worth listening to – all were sewn with humour, as that was his way.

Rob's life was dedicated to others less fortunate than himself and even when in the direst of health – still, it was always about the other person. Because of his, and Julie's want to support others, they left a legacy that helped thousands of challenged people to rise and achieve in the quest for happiness and self-value.

Rob was a great man (oh, he would scoff at that), but his greatest trait was one that towered above all his achievements – his attitude. Even when the worst seemed to call the loudest, Rob was happy and positive.

In this book, I discuss a concept taught by the Native American's of "Calling your Happiness". Rob did this naturally, he was always happy. Yes, he would acknowledge that his physical condition could not be worse and spoke about a time when he had a body that he could trust. But even so, Rob called happiness and it touched us all. His body may have disintegrated, but his mind worked happiness, was positive and full love.

His philosophy, *Life may not be the party you hoped for, but while you are here you might as well dance* fitted Rob well, as dance he did.

Rob, you inspire me. All I can give in return is love. It is appropriate that this book is dedicated to you.

Pat Grayson

THE INTELLIGENCE

a state of equanimity

S U I C I D E ... F R I D A Y 9 : 3 1 PM

Stevie was not sure if it was a coma or delirium that he had slipped into…
but it was good… Am I dead? He was glad to end his life here, wherever
here was – it was gentle – all was foggy. Then he remembered…

His mind recalled the preparation – twenty-five aspirins and a bottle
of whiskey should do the trick, so his research indicated. *Funny, I don't
even like whiskey.*

After most of the pill solution and three quarters of the whiskey he
was floaty. Yet there was still the driving voice that said more… more
tablet solution… more whiskey.

∞

SATURDAY 11:15 AM

Mrs Jones knocked on the door, "Stevie are yah there luvie?"

After a few seconds she knocked again, "Stevie...Open up...Come on Stevie... open up, I know you're there... yah cars in the drive."

That was an hour ago, and now again she tried, but no response.

Worried, she went for help.

∞

SATURDAY 12:25 PM

"I hope he's fine," said Mrs Jones to the building manager, "he's been depressed of late."

"Let's see what we can do", the manager said.

∞

Stevie, ever organized, had secured the door from the inside with the barrel bolt he had installed – he did not want to be rescued.

He chose Aspirin because most medical personal have little experience with it. They also underestimate its severity. Several hours on the Internet gave him the answers he needed. He learnt that in most cases of drug overdose, there is a treatment that can quickly nullify the drug and stabilize the patient. He learnt that the treatment was governed by the ascertaining of which drug had been used. To make identification difficult he had discarded the packaging in a garbage can up the road. He also dissolved the tablets in water to eliminate brand marks, in case he did not finish them all. He knew that any delay in identifying the drug would enhance his death. Death would be as a result of complications from the acidosis build up, usually resulting in cardiac arrest or central nervous system breakdown. Stevie knew that with the ingestion of the entire solution the chances of him being saved were reduced. He shuddered and consumed the rest of the solution.

∞

Confused, Stevie saw his body…There seemed to be two of him. The him, looking at the scene, and the one on the settee.

Through the door he saw Mrs Jones trying to open the door, calling, "Stevie, are yah there? Stevie, are yah okay? Let me in Stevie." After a time, he saw her retreat down the hall.

Trying to rationalize what was happening he observed all that was around him; he emitted a light that illuminated the dark room. At first things were hazy but became clearer. He realized that he was not standing on the floor but floating above it. There was also a kind of vibration that pulsed through his body. At this stage he noticed an elasticized cord that was attached to his head and the body on the settee. Although the pressure was not strong, it was a constant, gentle pull towards the body as if the body wanted to snap his other form into its physical self. Stevie resisted this as he did not want to go back into his body.

The floating was like a ping pong ball in water and difficult to get used to, especially the defying of gravity. This was too unnatural and he kept questioning if this was really happening or an effect of the alcohol and tablets.

∞

Still wondering if he was alive or dead, he looked around at his surroundings. It was weird but cosy – a large tunnel. The walls were cloud-like, remoulding shape and size with each moment. But it was the shafts of light that amazed him, dazzling white. He realized that it was the light that gave the cosy feeling. As he stared, he wondered where the tunnel led to, when he heard a voice, "It leads to more light and love".

Stevie looked towards where the voice came from. He became aware of a man staring at him. Strange man, he thought. Is he real?

"Yes, I'm real, well as real as real," he heard his mind say.

Stevie thought the aspirins and whiskey were playing with his mind.

"I'm real and you do see me, the drugs and alcohol have no effect on you here."

Stevie's mind raced. *This person reads my mind and plants thoughts in it. What does he mean over here?* He looked around, and saw that the shafts of light hung like drapes, and softened things. There was nothing harsh here.

"It's called telepathy. Everyone uses it on this side. Speech as used on Earth is cumbersome."

Stevie looked back to this strange man. He looked African but was tiny. What made him look even smaller was that from the hip upwards, his torso was virtually horizontal to the ground. For support he used a small crooked stick that he probably picked up in the bush somewhere. His face was tiny and pinched, as if the meat has been sucked out of it. Perched on his head was a checked hat, the type he had seen in photos or movies of older times. He wore a checked jacket, which was a different colour and clashed with the hat. Dark baggy pants completed the strange outfit.

Stevie's eyes went back to the face. So wrinkled, it looked like the hide of an elephant.

The man laughed at this.

The eyelids were narrow as if they had squinted into the sun too many times and had a slightly oriental look about them. The eyeballs were brown with large, red spider-web veins criss-crossing the white. High protruding cheek bones made the face appear even more shrivelled.

Once again, the man laughed, it was high pitched and musical. The laugh, or rather the crackle, was infectious, and the face became even more pinched, if that was possible.

Stevie became quiet and lapsed back into the sad and dejected mind set he had before the tablets and whiskey.

"That's what got you into the state that your life became," said the African to Stevie's mind.

"What the bloody hell are you talking about?" said Stevie aloud. He was not going to use this telepathy crap.

"Sadness, dejection, remorse, and the worst of all, self-pity," replied the African.

Stevie ignored this and louder than necessary asked, "What do you know about the state of my life?"

The crusty old face broke into another crackling chuckle but said nothing.

Stevie tried to pretend that the African was not there, but could not hide his curiosity, "Who are you?"

"My name is Weishka, and I am, or was, of the San people of the Kalahari in Africa. I was what you would call a witch doctor but we would prefer to be known as a sangoma or shaman – a spiritual healer." He paused for a while as if to let this information settle, and then continued, "I have come to help you. That is if you are ready to stop wallowing in self-pity". This was said in a kindly way.

Must be the drugs, Stevie thought, but said, "How can you help me? I don't want to be helped."

Weishka considered before sending his thoughts across, "I can show you the way to a better life."

Stevie's voice was shaky, "Life sucks and I don't want to go back again. Besides, I killed my kid… You… you won't send me back, will you?"

"No, I won't interfere with your life. It is your choice if you go back or finish crossing over. You have free will."

"Crossing over, what do you mean by that? Am I dead or not dead?"

"Yes, you are dead, and no you are not. You are in the tunnel of light that links physical life with the life of spirit. I have come to help you make your decision to continue or return to your body and physical life."

Stevie looked up and down the tunnel and thought to himself, I don't want to return.

Weishka said, "Good, use the thought process, it goes faster and there is no confusion."

Stevie sighed, "Why would I want to go back? Right now, I feel light and free and don't have a care in the world…other than being forced to go back."

It only took Stevie's mind a second to create this thought, and as soon as he had, Weishka's reply was immediate. In fact, it was so fast Stevie was startled. "The reason why you feel so light is because you are out of your physical or material body. It is your etheric body that you now enjoy."

"Marvellous, you can keep my body… I have no further use for it." But then changed the subject and thought, "Hey, what did you mean when you mentioned free will?"

"On Earth humans have the choice to go in any direction of their own choosing. This is called free will. For instance, you chose to live the fear-based negative life that you lived so far. Fear is usually the result of doubt… Do you doubt yourself?"

Stevie ignored the question, so Weishka continued, "You could just as easily decide to be more upbeat and happier. It was also your choice to end it. We on this side are not allowed to interfere with your free will. This applies from the time you are born to the time when you re-join us in the light plane. If we interfere with your free will, you would not grow and learn. Always, there is free will."

Stevie was getting better at handling the speed of the telepathy. They could have a conversation in only a few seconds. No sooner a thought was conceived, the reply had been received. Much like a computer hard disk that processes massive volumes of data instantly.

Weishka hearing Stevie's thoughts offered, "When telepathy is the means of communication there are no lies. There can't be, as we can see into each other's minds. I can see into yours, and when you improve your skill, you will be able to see into mine. So, there can't be any untruths. Nor can there be any ego or superiority… Imagine if all discussion and thought was conducted this way. Politicians would be more accountable, as would be business managers as deceit would be seen. There could be no betrayal."

Stevie was not interested in this discussion and so asked, "Do you ever take off your hat and jacket?"

"What, and be under dressed?"

Stevie ignored the joke so the old man thought, "I can appear any way I like. Most of us helpers adopt one of our favourite incarnations. The one that I am representing to you had no clothes and many times in the bitter winters we got cold, and so I guess I wear these as a sort of comfort ... But they're fun. I like the brightness." This was said with a bright smile.

"If you're a… what did you call yourself?"

"A San, of the Kalahari."

"A San, how come you speak so well? Not like a bushman?"

"Like the incarnation and clothes that I chose, I chose this form of English to make it easier for you to understand me."

"Oh," was all Stevie thought.

"We really do not have any form over here so we adopt a form for new arrivals. You also don't have a form here. You just think you do."

Stevie did not want to enter into this conversation about any of this stuff and remained silent.

The old man just stood there, patiently leaning on his stick.

"Why do you need the stick? What I mean is… what's wrong with your back that you need the stick?"

"Buffalo."

Changing the subject Weishka asked, "Would you like to see how you are getting on in your physical body?"

"What do you mean," asked Stevie.

"Just as I suggested, let's look at your body".

"I …I guess it wouldn't do any harm."

∞

…No sooner than it had been thought, Stevie found himself in his flat, hovering just below the ceiling.

Emotionless, he surveyed his body. His legs were spread on the settee, his trunk sprawled towards the floor. His face lay on the carpet, left side down. His mouth open, like a mullet, dribbling onto the carpet. What was most disconcerting was that his right eye was open – the blank stare of a doll's eye. Not a pretty sight he thought. He was grateful that Weishka was silent.

He looked around the small neat apartment. He had given it a 'spring' clean as part of his preparation. He did not care about being thought of as a responsible man, it was part of his ritual of death. As he scrubbed and polished, his mind was on life, and a cleansing, before death. As he cleaned, he was in no hurry, it would happen soon enough.

The whiskey bottle lay on the floor. The remaining contents too low to spill out.

He wanted to cross the room to have a closer look at his body. Suddenly, it was as if the room and the Stevie on the settee were pulled towards him. He jumped with fright as the coffee table that was between him and the couch passed through him as if he was made of smoke. The pulling stopped as the settee was directly in front of him. He tried to touch his body but his hand went through it.

Stevie heard a noise and saw Mrs Jones through the door with a man in overalls carrying a box of tools. He saw and heard the effort to break open the door and chuckled to himself when he saw his barrel bolt resist the effort. Mrs Jones, wringing her hands on her apron looked on with concern. Finally, with the aid of a crow bar and good shoulder strength from the building manager, the door gave in.

Stevie was about to hide but realized Mrs Jones or the man could not see him. In fact, the man walked right through him. This was an odd sensation as if a molasses goo passed through him but was gone when the man was on the other side of the room.

Twenty minutes later the ambulance arrived.

THE PARAMEDICS ...
SATURDAY 12:58 PM

The paramedic tried to resuscitate Stevie. With no response he shook his head to Mrs Jones and mouthed, "Almost no pulse. He's in a coma."

He checked for kidney damage, knowing the longer the time from ingestion to treatment, the greater the chance of kidney failure.

He laid Stevie on the floor, and called the other paramedic, "look for packaging or samples of what this guy took. I see he imbibed a bit of whiskey." To try and shock the heart into a stronger beat, with well-practiced hands, he applied the wires of the defibrillator to Stevie's heart area. After double checking, he pressed the plunger. There was no improvement, the heart was pumping but only just.

Mrs Jones knelt next to him. She remembered how kind he was to her, "Can I carry your shopping Mrs Jones – let me do that for you Mrs Jones..." An intelligent boy she thought, and not pretentious. Good looking with those blue eyes and black hair, cut in the modern way. His slightly almond-shaped eyes set in a face of pale, clear skin and full lips give him a sensitive appearance.

Even like this he is clean with freshly washed jeans and t-shirt. Poor thing is only about twenty-six and he does this to himself. "What's this she said, as she picked up a crimpled page that had been torn out of a notepad. It had been under Stevie's body, as she straightened it out, the words jumped out at her.

Goodbye Cruel World

Sorry, not very original but that's all my blurry mind can come up with at the moment. A third of the liquid, and half of the whiskey is gone, and I am starting to feel pretty wobbly of mind.

I didn't want to write one of these but thought I'd better so no one gets in trouble. I did this to myself, I'm the guilty party. Seems, that I always have been the guilty party!

I can't do it any longer, living this lie of a life... just too much of a battle. I simply do not want to continue with it. Even the substances I take don't make it better any more not since that thing happened. Anyway, all I seem to do is battle.

Doctors; I forbid you to treat me. This missive of mine is, I think you call it, a 'Care Directive'. You do not keep me alive –

do you hear???

Sorry Mrs Jones to do this to you, and sorry you have to see me this way. There is money in the top draw to pay for the door damage that is likely to occur. I liked you, you were always nice to me.

Mandy, oh Mandy. Don't know what to say. What can I say? I am so sorry for how it ended up. Yes, it was my fault, what I did to our... I just can't bear it. You were the best thing that ever happened to me and I did what I did to you.

xxx.

Paramedic took his phone out and took a photo of it for their records and said, "You must leave this for the police as they will need to investigate. I see that it is not signed. But they will have their experts examine the writing against other writing of his that must be here. Do you recognise the writing Mrs Jones?"

Mrs Jones re looked at the paper, "Yes, that's his writing, I have seen it a hundred times." Then, perhaps leave it on that table and show it to the police when they get here. We will have them called, you won't have to worry."

With heavy breathing and tears in her eyes, she got up off the floor and gently placed the note on the side table, as if a sacred document.

∞

The paramedic could not declare the patient dead, only the doctor on duty at the General Hospital could do that. He did the standard procedures of taking control of the breathing, maintained correct blood pressure and put Stevie on a ventilator. He inserted an IV to ensure the stabilizing of fluid and electrolytes, controlling adrenalin before putting him into the ambulance. The paramedic climbed in the back of the ambulance to continue with CPR.

∞

In Earth terms, it was not long before Stevie saw the paramedic shake his head. This disorientated him, I have seen enough, he thought.

Weishka let Stevie process his confusion before returning to the tunnel of light.

∞

When Stevie was more composed, he said aloud, almost as if to himself, "That was ugly… But I still don't want to go back."

"The choice to return is yours… But I would like to offer you a challenge."

Stevie was wary, "What sort of challenge? I don't want any challenges. I'd prefer to be on my way, along this tunnel."

Weishka said in a firm voice, "You know by dying, the fear that engulfed you will have had its way, right to the end – and won?"

"Oh great, mind games with a spook."

Weishka ignored the remark and continued, "A life wasted because you did not have the knowledge to pull yourself together."

"It's Easy for you to say that."

Weishka answered, "I have had my time on Earth. I can tell you that the hot and dry sands of the Kalahari sapped the life out of us. We lived with a belly that was more often empty than full and where danger sprang from every rock and crevice. I know hardship... But when it was my time, I looked life firmly in the eye and did the best I could. It was a life worth living, and so can yours be."

Stevie did not want this conversation but immediately received another transmission from Weishka. "That's right, all your life you ran from this conversation and where did it get you, sleeping pills, whiskey and a soft exit."

"Why does my death worry you so much?"

"Because if you knew of the alternative way to live, your life could be happy. You have nothing to lose by listening to me".

Sullen, Stevie said nothing but after a time blurted out, "Okay, what's this challenge?"

Weishka's thoughts were quick to come, "I could lecture you on those alternative ways of being for hours but you would probably not believe me. Experience is the best teacher, so I would like you to go on a 'journey of learning'. This will be on the etheric plane, but it will feel as real to you as if on the material plane. By experiencing this journey, you will be better able to decide if you want to return to your life on the third dimension. As with all life, there will be ups and downs, good and bad. But this time it will be different as you will learn a different set of rules to live by."

THE HOSPITAL ...
SATURDAY 1:22 PM

Saturday night at the Gen is mayhem as Stevie is rushed through the emergency room.

"What have we got here?" asked an overworked doctor in hospital garb that looked like it had been worn for a week. Prematurely grey hair, cut close to the skin made him look much older than his forty-two years.

"We think an attempted suicide," said the paramedic. "Comatose, virtually no pulse, have kept him on the ventilator."

"Rose… here," shouted the doctor. "A plump and mature nurse with the name tag of Rosemary hurried across.

"Leave that and get this patient on the ward's ventilator ASAP. Call me when ready."

"Yes, Dr Ritchie."

Before heading off the doctor asked the paramedic, "You said you think he tried to commit suicide… Were you able to bring back any drugs or samples this guy took?"

"Whiskey, there was an almost empty bottle. We had a good look around for drugs or boxes of tabs but saw nothing. Seems like he took more than just the whisky. The door was locked on the inside with a barrel bold that would keep him undisturbed for some time. But have a look at this". The paramedic fished his phone out of his pocket and bought to screen the note that Stevie wrote, and showed the doctor.

The doctor quickly scanned the note and nodded his head in acknowledgement of the Health Directive. He would ignore this until it was proven to be the patient's hand writing. He then asked, "How well did you look for packaging?"

"My partner went through garbage tins, shopping bags, everything but there weren't any."

Okay, thought the doctor as he looked at Stevie, you really wanted to do this didn't you?

∞

Weishka continued the conversation as if Stevie was interested and asked, "Do you believe in Karma?" Stevie said nothing, but Weishka continued anyway. "You will learn karma exists and you will have created a type of karma by ending your life if you don't go back. You know from your time on Earth that you had many things to learn but if you sacrifice this life before you master those lessons then in your next incarnation you will be confronted with the same lessons. It will be karma that you would create for yourself."

Stevie thought to himself, "This is rubbish, and there is nothing that a journey can teach me."

"Yes, it will. You have already learnt two things since being here. The first is telepathy. You did not think this possible before, yet you have been using it in our short time together. You can grow this skill on the Earth plane if you focus correctly.

The other thing you have learnt is that there is no death, not in the real sense, and that there is an afterlife. Although you have not had time to think of the consequences of this, it should be obvious that there are different levels of life. This should indicate an organizing power behind life. You have also learnt that you can instantaneously return back and forth to the physical and non-physical as you did a few moments ago".

Stevie said nothing but took in what was said.

The old man continued, "You can call that organizing power God if you wish, there are many names for it but names are meaningless. I call it, 'The Intelligence'. Some people call it Love with a capital L, as love is the strongest power there is."

Stevie's face showed his lack of interest, "I don't know if I believe in God or whatever *you* want to call it."

Weishka continued, "You may not, but when I look into your mind, I see more clutter than a child's bedroom after the child plundered the toy boxes. The clutter represents questions about the riddles of life. Which of those many questions would you like to have an answer to now?"

Stevie raised his eyebrows, "Sure, then why are we here, especially when life can be so shit?"

"Good question. Look at it this way – there is intelligence in animal migration, cell division and biology, as there is in all of nature. This is the Intelligence that I refer. This Intelligence is the creative and organizing power behind all forms of life. And, there would be no intelligence in us if there were no intelligence behind the universe. It is the intelligence behind the universe that you call God. Over here we have a reverence for that Intelligence. So, in answer to your question as to why we are here; you on Earth, and us entities over here, it is to become more at one with the Intelligence."

Stevie said nothing but his mind raced.

"So," Weishka continued, "If our lives were controlled by fate, what would be the reason for living or the purpose of this grand experiment of the universe? Where would the learning and growth come from and how would mankind develop? What would be in it for The Intelligence? There would be no reason, but if you look at it from the point of aligning with it through growth and development then it makes a lot of sense. But for you on Earth, by accepting the principles and aligning with it, your life is more likely to flow as you would like it."

Stevie was thoughtful before asking, "How will aligning myself with this Intelligence make my life better?"

Weishka smiled, he knew the question would come. "The Intelligence is obviously the creative force. All things that are created are an expression of that Intelligence. You, therefore, are an aspect of it. By deduction you have aspects of the Intelligence. By recognizing this you align with it and by doing so you are able to utilize those aspects. But before I give you time to think about this, there is something else that you need to understand and that is that you asked for these teachings. Not consciously but on a soul level."

"Asked, on a soul level, what do you mean?"

"Your soul understood that on a conscious level you were not learning. It could see that your life was uncomfortable and disruptive. On a conscious and personality level you were weak and wanted to end it. As you said – I'm out of here'… But for now, enough talking. I shall leave you so that you can consider what I have said. But before I go there are two things that I need to say. The first is, because of the condition of your physical body, I suggest you go and check on it every so often. That's why I wanted you to have a look as you did. All you have to do is to think of going to your body and you will be there.

The other thing that I encourage you to do is to re-experience parts of your life. Over here you are able to backtrack in time to see past events unfold. This is good for learning but you have no power to change them, just observe them."

E M E R G E N C Y   R O O M ...
S A T U R D A Y   1 : 3 6   P M

Dr Ritchie worked swiftly – he took the pulse and placed a contracting bandage around Stevie's arms to do a CUP blood pressure test. At the same time, he looked for needle marks – at least he is not that type of addict, he thought.

"Is he going to make it Doctor?" asked Rose.

"Doubt it… he is only four on the Glasgow Coma Scale"

"Such a waste, he must only be in his mid-twenties." She wondered what would cause a good-looking young man to want to end his life. He is tall and slender, much like my William was. She knew what the Glasgow Coma Scale signified, it is the level of consciousness of a person. Zero is considered dead, fifteen is normal consciousness. A four is not good… she willed it to rise up the scale.

Ritchie said, "He's in no man's land between life and death… virtually no pulse." Shining his torch into Stevie's eyes he said, "Seems to be no brain activity…. and now he has dropped to three on the Glasgow Coma Scale. Still, let's watch him for a few hours. Keep him on the ventilator and apply low coma inducement. Feed him 10 MCGs per minute and see how he responds. We may have to increase it. Take a blood sample and send to the lab. Try to ID what this foolish boy took."

Rose asked, "Are we to send him to ICU?"

"No, probably a waste of time. He can stay here for the time being."

∞

Be good to watch TV, Stevie thought… and forget all of this stuff.

I know, I'll go and visit my body and when in the ward see if I can watch TV there. Old Elephant-Hide face said I can go back and watch part of my life, and TV is a good place to start. Hope there are chips to nibble on…

∞

"This is a waste of time. Not having any physical power, I can't channel-hop. There's no sport, too many ads, and soaps, which bore me. How depressing… hate hospitals with a passion.

Wanting to move away, he crossed the ward and chose a chair by the window. As he was about to sit, he realised there was an object on the chair and got up to have a look. A crooked stick. What's this doing here? It then struck him that it was Weishka's stick, which literally said, "I'm watching you". Stevie chuckled,

That crafty old bugger.

His mind wandered to a time when he was eleven. He liked school and the challenge of wanting to come first. Most years he did but since Mandy Piper arrived there was someone to knock him off his perch. He didn't mind this, in fact he liked the challenge.

He remembered the day she came and the Headmaster bought her into the class and introduced her. At that stage Stevie did not like girls, but she was sort of cute; longish blond hair, big white teeth encased in braces, and a band of freckles that crossed her nose. He smiled at the memory.

The teacher said, "Go and sit with that boy with dark hair, his name is Steven Jardine." Stevie blushed and squirmed in his seat. He wished the teacher had her sit elsewhere but the seat next to him was the only one vacant.

When she sat down Stevie kept his face facing straight ahead but swivelled his eyes to watch her. She seemed fussy in the way she placed her pens, pencils and ruler on the desk. He pretended that she wasn't there but when she quietly elbowed him in his side, he was forced to look at her. She smiled as she offered him a sweet. As sweets were forbidden in class, it tasted even nicer.

From that moment on they were inseparable. They competed in class but studied together. They competed in athletics, and when playing marbles or handball at break. Months later, with the year coming to an end, the results board showed them both having the same number of stars – thirty-five. Their closest rival only had twenty-seven.

Stevie did not mind if Mandy claimed the class prize but he was going to give it his best shot. He knew that with the coming tests for arithmetic, spelling and reading they would both get 100% for all three, but thought, I can beat her with the project. The subject was on Dinosaurs, a favourite of his. He fancied Tyrannosaurus Rex, which he called T-rex and studied them for hours. He had collated all his material, and now it was to be handed in the next day. Tonight, he was to finish it and neatly write out the words. Everything was organized and ready for this last stage.

Coming home he went straight to his room to start. No sooner did he get everything out, Joe, his Foster dad barged into his room – with a beer in hand bellowed, "Get outside and cut the weeds that's growen against the fence."

"Joe, I have an urgent project to finish and it must be handed in tomorrow morning. Please can I do it tomorrow afternoon?"

"Get the hell out into the garden and do as I say. Do you want me to take the strap to you? Damn book worm. You spend too much time in your room with books. They won't get you anywhere. Look at me, I have never read a book in me life and I do well."

Stevie looked at the dirty clothes and bulging beer belly and knew pleading would be a waste of time. He tried anyway, "Please Joe, Can't I… His words were smothered when Joe made a move towards him, whilst starting to undo his belt and so Stevie ran towards the back door.

"And make sure yah do a proppa job," yelled Joe, after him, "and don't come back in until it's finished, yah hear?"

The house they lived in was the oldest in the suburb. The wooden paling fence had many missing palings. In one section it lent over at an awkward angle. It was long and would take several hours.

When he finally came in it was dark. Doris, his foster mother scolded, "Now get into the bath and clean up before you have your dinner. And don't give me no lip or I'll send you back to that orphanage."

Stevie bathed and ate his dinner. Once he washed the dishes he was told to get to bed. After they had gone to bed he worked on his project. His room wasn't really a bedroom; it was more of a store room. There were no curtains on the glass door, so if he turned on the light it would have shone into their bedroom. He did the project by the window, from the light of the outside street lamp.

The next day, in full daylight Stevie could see that he had made several mistakes, "Damn, damn, damn, I hate you Joe," he cursed as he walked to school.

A week later the project results were announced; Mandy got three stars, Peter Wentworth received two and Stevie one. Mandy came to Stevie and said, "I'm amazed that I won, you are much better at projects than me."

He never told her why he got a low mark as he congratulated her.

At the end of the school year, Joe walked into Stevie's room holding Stevie's school report, "You spend all you bloody time in books and don't even come first. What's wrong with yah?"

And now, and sitting in the ward, Stevie resentment rose as he thought of Joe and Doris.

∞

"Well, are you willing to undergo the journey?"

"You damn well know what the answer is." Hating the pressure, right at that moment, all he wanted was the security of some alcohol. His stomach squirmed, like it did when Mandy sat next to him all those years ago. If he returned his life would immediately be crap. But this journey seemed better than the known. With control he said, "I have another question. Will you be with me?"

"I have always been with you. You just chose not to see me. Yes, I will be with you when you need me."

E M E R G E N C Y   R O O M ...
S A T U R D A Y 8 : 1 8 P M

"Calling Doctor Ritchie, calling Doctor Ritchie, please call in – this is an emergency.

Calling Doctor…"

"Ritchie here, what's wrong?"

"Doctor, there's an issue with patient Jardine in bed 85B. Can you attend?"

"Be there in thirty seconds."

It took thirty-five seconds for Ritchie to round the curtain and ask Rose, "What's wrong?"

"He's had a seizure and also vomited, but very little came out… And, his Glasgow reading is down another point".

This was a complication that Ritchie expected but hoped to avoid. Acute, Respiration, Distress, Syndrome, ARDS for short. The seizure could be from elevated acidity and would have caused the vomiting. He needed to check for lung inflammation.

"Has the lab returned with the blood tests yet?" he asked.

"No, not yet."

"Call them and put a rocket up their backsides, we don't have time to play games…and organize a lung inflammation test."

Rose hurried off to the Nurse's desk...

∞

Mandy Piper was in her lab, leaning back in her chair examining a DNA extraction of fungi in molecular form. With her feet resting on her desk, her white coat hung to the floor, too engrossed to care. Mandy was a consultant to the National Museum and wondered if their specimens would have been better preserved if this method had been around when the specimens had been found. The extraction had been created from a new method of field preservation.

The ringing of the phone startled her. At first, she ignored it but its insistence interrupted her concentration, and so with a sigh of frustration, rocked forward to a normal seated position and picked up the phone, and said, "Dr Piper, how can I help you…"

Twenty seconds later she dropped the phone and rushed out the door.

∞

Weishka said, "There is a condition that we have no control over and to a degree nor do you. That is… if your physical body extinguishes before your etheric journey is over you will not be able to go back to your body and you will have to continue along the tunnel of light."

"If my body extinguishes, as you put it, why can't I go back, after all, are we not living some sort of magic here?"

"If the life force leaves your body, your etheric form will not be able to return to your body."

Stevie said, "Good, that's what I want, but wanted confirmation. So all I have to do is to hang out over here until my body gives up the fight and all is good?"

"That's one way of looking at it. We will not encourage you either way… but remember, you are doing this as a journey of learning and it is pointless if you are not open to the experience. Your journey will seem as real as if it is in your material world – that is, that all things, although ethereal, will appear real and solid."

Stevie's first thought was, who cares about learning? I'm for the tunnel. But like a child who quickly knew his thoughts were known, guiltily thought, well…so what?

Weishka laughed, releasing the tension, "I may be your elder by a thousand years or so but you don't have to recover your poise with me. Anyway, about the journey, as I said before, you can go back to your body at any time but if you go back no wiser than when you came across here then your life is likely to be much the same as it was."

"So, let me get this straight...I can go back to my life any time I want, but if I go back before passing the grade then I get the same old crap? But if I don't get back before my body expires then I continue what I started, and go up the pipe...But if I stay here a while and have amazing learning, then like a wonder pill, all will be fine. Is that right?"

"Yes, that's right."

"So, I can continue along this tunnel or return to my life?"

"Yes."

"When do I have to decide?"

"Over here there is no time, so there is no hurry. But on the other side..."

"What?" Stevie asked with panic.

"Well, as I said, once your physical body is clinically dead the choice is gone and you remain here until your next incarnation... to continue what you were to learn this time around."

"Well, that's a no brainer, because I ain't going back. But what am I to do on this journey?"

"Be aware, and follow your heart."

"Oh great," mocked Stevie. "Follow my heart? I have no idea what you mean."

"You have free will, use it and start to learn trust."

"How long will the journey to take?"

"It will take as long as it needs to."

"Okay, how do I know what my heart tells me – after all, it told me to end it, using whiskey and pills as fuel." Stevie guffawed at his own wit.

Weishka ignored this, "You are going to learn that what you ask for can be received. You do this by knowing that you are an aspect of The Intelligence."

With seemingly nothing to lose Stevie asked, "Where do I get my ticket for this mysterious journey?"

∞

"Good," said Weishka, knowing all along Stevie would undertake it. "Now you need to decide where the journey is to take place. So, all jokes aside, you must focus. I want you to close your eyes and visualize the journey you want."

Stevie had always loved the bush. It seemed to make more sense than cities and so if he was to undertake this journey, he thought it would be much nicer doing it in the bush. He remembered a documentary about two men who hiked down a mountain range. It took them months to complete. To Stevie it had seemed a worthwhile goal, in the bush. Yes, a hike in those mountains.

He looked at Weishka and thought, "Do you see it in my mind?"

Weishka's smiled, "Yes, the second you did!"

"Well, is it okay?"

"You're talking to a Bushman of the Kalahari, and the Kalahari is not all desert. There is lots of bush and the bush offers much to learn from. We roamed it all our lives and loved every inch of it… But listen to me. As you requested it will be a journey in the bush and although it will seem real, in as much as the trees will seem solid, and there will be normal climatic conditions… you will feel hot or cold accordingly, you will get tired and will need to sleep. If you fall over you are just as likely to hurt yourself as in normal life."

"Why can't it be like it is here with weightlessness and light?"

"For you to get the most benefit from your journey of self-nourishment it must be as real as your life on Earth. There will be times when it will be uncomfortable."

'Uncomfortable' seemed ominous to Stevie.

"As the journey is etheric," the old man went on "— do you know what I mean by etheric?

"Something spooky, I bet," said Stevie.

"Your world is material, meaning that everything seems solid to you. We will leave that for now but other realms that can't be seen by mankind are etheric or not solid matter."

"If I can't see this etheric realm, how can I believe it exists?"

"Well, you are talking to me in the non-material world… do you believe it?"

"To be honest I don't know what to believe."

"You also have seen your body, whilst being external from it, haven't you?"

"Yes, and freaky it was but I still don't know if I believe this. It is so difficult getting used to. I am here in this etheric experience, yet my thoughts are normal and I seem to be the same and so have difficulty marrying the differences." He became quiet to give Weishka a chance to speak and help him, but then could not help himself when he posed the question, "Is life an illusion then?"

Wanting to let Stevie find his own answer Weishka returned the question, "Do you think life is an illusion?"

Faltering at first, Stevie started, "I… … I think it could be an illusion. … Of course, the illusion seems real to us because of the debt we are in or the happiness we can feel."

"Go on", encouraged Weishka.

"Probably the main reason that illusion is so real is because of our emotions. We do not seem to ever be without emotions; happy is an emotion, and fear… of being in debt or the result of being in debt is another emotion. We experience hundreds of emotions every day. They are either positive emotion or negative emotions. I think I lived mostly with the negative."

Weishka cut in and said, "You, and all humans create your own reality. You do this intentionally or not.

But here is the important point, by creating your own reality you manipulate or develop the illusion. Conversely, the illusion you live in, is a reflection of what you have created".

"Hang on", Stevie said louder than was necessary, "I hear what you say but have difficulty getting my head around that one".

You will in time, just be open to it. But let me continue. Because you live in illusion, it is an empowering thought to know that you can manipulate the illusion by creating your reality. By controlling the negative emotions, you go a long way towards developing a better illusion.

What do you think of this now?"

Shrugging, he left the space open for Weishka to continue.

"What I said was for you and each individual, but there is a collective illusion, which governs the state of the planet. What I mean by this is that the planet, let's not get complex and talk about the universe, is in its current predicament because of the collective emotions of humankind.

As each of you seem to be predominantly negatively-emotionally charged, this is reflected in a fear based and negatively-emotionally charged world. I think you will agree that the world is in bad shape. But the good news is, by changing your own negatively charged emotion to that of being positively charged, you contribute to a better world.

Being the optimist, I believe we can do this, but it will take every one of you.

Perhaps the main difference between this side and the material is that on this side you have a greater sense of who you are in your privileged place in the universe. I say privileged because when you understand the love and acceptance of life then you can't help but be grateful. But on the Earth plane it is not as obvious and so you have to look for it. Some do, as even though they may have mortgages and family, work and issues, they still have a strong sense of their privileged place in the universe. Sadly, there are many that don't and are far from that sense of privilege. The gratitude is akin to love..."

Stevie's mind wandered when Weishka said, "love" ...He instantly thought of Mandy and the first time they made love. They had not seen each other for four or five years, she had gone to University to study anthropology. Joe forced Stevie to leave school and support the family by working. About three months earlier they found themselves at the same party. Both had partners in tow – virtually forgotten. Stevie was shocked at the depth of his feeling for her. Mandy always knew Stevie was the one.

It was at her place. They had just finished a leisurely supper. Both had contributed to its creation, Mandy made the starters and the pudding, Stevie cooked the lobster and sautéed vegetables. After the meal, they took their glasses of red wine and went to sit outside in the cool, and to take in the stars. Sitting cross-legged on the blanket Stevie wanted to take things slowly and so admired the night sky. Mandy sitting opposite had other ideas, not being caught in the culture of false modesty, where the woman pretends to be chase, she pulled his face towards her and kissed him deeply. Letting him go she pulled off her top. Stevie studied her in the moonlight, taking in the straight torso, wide shoulders, and petite breasts; he pulled her towards him…

"Hmmm, excuse me…" Weishka interrupted. "Remember me? We are having a conversation and your mind seems to have wandered… a bit. Now, you were about to say something?"

"Sorry, you were not meant to see that."

Weishka smiled and said, "It's forgotten already. Please continue."

Stevie knew Weishka was pulling his leg, but continued anyway, "I was one of those that did not look, wasn't I?"

"You were."

"If I was like that, why was I not taught or shown where I was going wrong?"

"You have to understand you are given free will to do as you please. It is your choice to see how you fit into the universe."

"Then why do some naturally see their place of privilege and some don't?"

"It is a choice; some feel grateful for life and all it has to offer. Others don't and tend to get lost in issues. Such as sneaking off to the hospital to watch TV…"

Stevie laughed about being caught out and simply said, "Nice one with the stick."

Weishka's chuckled, "Old Elephant-Hide face, eh."

"Anyway, to continue, things that seem important are not really important when one considers things on a cosmic level. To put it simply, some just do not understand what are the important things in life."

"I'll need to think about it for a while."

Stevie was quiet for some time but felt Weishka's question to him. "You ready?"

"Ready for what?"

"To start your journey."

"Hang on, I have lots of questions to ask. What about food and hiking equipment? Where do I sleep, do I take water? What about…"

Weishka interrupted him, "You will receive all that you require by trusting. You will draw it to yourself."

Stevie was panic-struck. Not normally so indecisive. Thinking of his options, he was instantly, back with his body in the Hospital. Looking at it, he was horrified – to go back to this and his dysfunctional life, or into the unknown. Neither were enticing. He thought of his childish behaviour with Mandy, and many other issues in his life… his child. Then, with the same avoidance, he knew he could not face it. Whatever lay at the end of the tunnel was to be his fate.

And with that, Stevie was whisked away at such speed that he had no idea of what was happening – flashes and swirling, form and no-form. It only seemed to last a second or two, or so he thought.

∞

The next thing he knew he was on a beach. Once gaining his equilibrium he took stock of his surroundings. The beach was lovely, but hell what now, he thought. He looked around to get his bearings. The sun was high and hot, the beach deserted, not a foot print in the sand, and not a sign of man ever having been there. He felt panic in his gut, and fear descended like a heavy cloud. Trying to raise his spirits he mumbled, guess no one will worry if I skinny-dip?

Wondering where he was to go, he remembered the conversation with Weishka, "Be aware and follow your heart. You have free will, use it, and start to learn trust. Feel the way."

What the hell does that mean, he wondered? And where do I sleep, I can't see any huts?

"Did you forget to visualize a hut?" joked Weishka.

Stevie said nothing but thought to himself, I knew that this was a bad idea.

Weishka continued the joke, "Without a hut, I guess that you will have to sleep outside."

Feeling insecure, Stevie asked, "And food… where is it? And what about fresh water? You said that these things will be provided."

"They will be, but only if you trust."

Stevie's irritation grew, "Trust who, trust what? What the hell do you mean trust?"

"It goes like this. We spoke about 'The Intelligence', and that you are an aspect of it. The Intelligence is obviously the Creative Force behind everything. You have to trust that it is there. You also have to trust that you are an aspect of it, in which case you must trust that you can also create. On Earth, people call this visualizing, manifesting, creating abundance, and all sorts of other terms. The concept is good, but does not normally work there. The reason is that they don't trust that the object of their vision will happen. They are locked in a mind-set of duality where The Intelligence is different to them. By believing in separateness, how can they manifest? They can't, is the answer."

With anger Stevie said, "Then I am likely to starve to death here because I don't understand any of this stuff."

"Stevie you have already learnt things that you could not have conceived of only a short time ago. I ask you to…"

"You mean that if I see myself as part of what you call 'The Intelligence' and then ask for things like food and believe that it will happen then it will happen?"

"Yes, it will, but it is not quite as straight forward as that."

"I knew it," moaned Stevie. "And what else, is there more?"

"Love. That's all, love." Weishka waited for Stevie's outburst. It was quick to come.

Stevie's words rushed out of him, "Don't you understand that love is the most difficult concept in the world to define? How do I all of a sudden be love? It's impossible."

"No, Stevie, it's not. Not when you understand it. Love is the spark of our being, our very essence. It is the most potent force there is and I promise you that if you complete this journey with an open mind, you will know what love is… But let me say this. You have said that you do not understand The Intelligence, nor do you understand love… could it be that Love and The Intelligence are one and the same?"

Stevie was stunned at this thought. Sensing the importance of this conversation he answered, "Yes it's possible but how can I know it to be as you say?"

Weishka smiled the gentlest smile that Stevie had seen from him so far. "It is so, but I can't prove it to you. Love is a noun where it is a state of being. Yes, it is followed up as a verb of doing… and it is also an adjective that describes a way of being. But remember, this journey is experiential and so you will have to prove it to yourself. Are you ready to give it a go?"

"I have no choice, do I?" grumbled Stevie. "Is there more I should know about?"

"No, not in the sense of other requirements. It is more of you understanding the way you receive. To give you an example, when you are supplied with something that you have wanted, it may not come in the way you asked for. For instance; let's say that you started a business and needed money to rent premises. You ask for that money. Three or four days later you get annoyed because the bag of money has not arrived. But yet, a friend may offers, "Why not come and start your business in my office? I have a spare room that you can use that's just gathering dust. I'm happy to help you and won't charge you. Besides, it'll be good to have someone else to chat to on occasions." What you ask for will come to you but it could be in a way that was not expected. But let's make a start. Now assuming the trust and the love are in place, to use an Earth term, you set the intent. When setting intent, you must use all of your senses."

At this time, Weishka held up a gnarled hand, which looked more like a claw, and counted off the steps. "These are; that you see it happening, hear it happening, feel it happening, smell it happening, and if possible even taste it happening." Then, indicating a sixth finger said, "Most important, you believe that it will happen because you trust.

You have to understand", continued Weishka, "how positive intent and The Intelligence combine to succeed in a given project. Work on it and the universe will work with you. Leave it to the unknown as far as results go, just go through the necessary movements. You are merely a link in the chain of causation. Fundamentally, all happens in the mind only. When you work with something whole-heartedly and steadily, it happens for it is the function of the mind to make things happen. In reality nothing is lacking and nothing is needed, all work is on the surface only, and The Intelligence does the rest. "You fine with this so far?"

Stevie was dubious but nodded his head.

"Good, now if you were to go on a hike in your other life, what would you need?"

Stevie thought, "Ummm… food and water… a backpack to carry everything in. A hat to keep the sun off my head and face. Perhaps sun block. Decent hiking shoes." When finished, he expectantly looked at Weishka, like a child would look at his mother after asking for an ice cream.

"Good," Weishka said. "Now close your eyes and start off with the first item on your list… food I think it was. See yourself with enough and arriving at the right time."

Stevie did not think that this would work but was aware that he needed to at least try to follow the processes or he would starve. On hikes he preferred fruit and nuts to starchy foods and focused on those. He ran the foods through his five senses, and did his best to believe.

"Now send love to your intent. Don't worry if it feels awkward. Send a warm smile to it."

Stevie did and found that it was easier to feel love than he realized. When he opened his eyes, he looked around for the bowl of fruit and nuts. Not seeing any he looked at Weishka with an expression that said, "Well, where is it?"

Weishka eyes crinkled with delight, "Just wait, it will come."

EMERGENCY ROOM ...
SUNDAY 1:25 AM

Things were quite in the ward. Once again Rose was at the foot of Jardine's bed. She finished her shift some time ago and should have gone. For the umpteenth time she checked the monitor and the instruments – blood pressure almost non-existent. She looked to see that the finger peg and line were okay. Then, she rolled him over onto his side to try and eliminate bed-sores from forming. Sighing to herself, she was worried, as most deaths occurred between 2.00 and 4.00 a.m. 'Why did he do this ... why?'

∞

The beach was a paradise, golden sand, deep blue sky, perfect temperature, and sparkling water. Stevie spent the rest of the day swimming and sunbathing. He tried not to think about the journey and wanted to enjoy himself. He would start his hike tomorrow. He remembered Weishka words… remain positive.

He headed around the rocky headland to explore the many rock pools. On the way he found a bottle that had been washed up onto the beach… the first sign on mankind. Picking it up he saw it was corked. "Hmmm, wonder if there's a note from a shipwrecked sailor?" The cork was tight but released okay. The bottle has some stale smelling sea water. He emptied it and gave it a good wash. Later he would fill it with fresh water from a creek he found. He had a drink from it and the water was lovely and cool.

∞

The tide was out but the pools had been topped up from waves that washed over them. Seemingly without a care in the world he spent several hours investigating the area. Wonder if the rest of the journey of learning will be as difficult as this?

Walking further, "Oh man, oysters, I love oysters. And mussels!"

For an hour he made a glutton of himself.

Feeling satisfied. He headed back to the beach to watch the sun set. For a time, it snuggled into the folds of the green hills beyond sinking below them, taking its warmth and light with it. He watched the colours and light as it changed every few seconds. Gold and orange clouds billowed, large and voluminous. Seagulls worked the water's edge, looking for one last morsel before the day retired; their little red stick-legs working overtime. There was one with a bunged-up leg, the claws pointed at right angles to its body. Yet, it hobbled and hustled with bravado. At one stage a worm or crab that Stevie could not see caused a commotion where three or four birds all squabbled at the same time. With flapping of wings and squawking, it is was the bird with the bunged-up leg that came away as the victor. … Interesting, Stevie though. The water's edge rippled the same gold and orange. Ducks, dark in the waning light sliced the air in their v-formation. Every so often one would honk.

"Lovely, isn't it? You could just sit and marvel…" Steve turned around to see Weishka lying in the sand next to him.

"Oh you. Where's my food… bedding and things?"

"You ate, didn't you?"

"What do you mean? I never got food from you?"

"What about the delicious seafood you gorged on this afternoon? Are you not satisfied?"

"That wasn't from you, they were there for the picking, and so I picked."

"Stevie, remember I said that sometimes the required item does not come in the form expected. You were amply supplied… be grateful."

"Besides, you must consider how you found your meal."

Stevie had not made a correlation between the seafood and the setting of his intent and so grudgingly conceded that it was possible that he was supplied. But asked, "What about a place to sleep and bedding?"

"Oh, you'll get on okay," was all Weishka said.

EMERGENCY ROOM ...
SUNDAY 2:46 AM

Rose sighed as there was still no change. Seeing that the lab results were not back, she called for them. Her voice carried more tension than necessary when she said, "...and don't forget the lung inflammation result – ASAP."

She slumped in the visitor's chair, something she would not normally do. The green walls of the ward not noticed, so deep was her thought. It was on another young man… Until, with a start, she realised that her mind had been miles away, when she should have been working. As she wiped away the tears, she quickly looked around to see if any of the nursing staff had seen her. She thought she had not been seen.

∞

Not taking any chances, Stevie thought he had better prepare a place to sleep. Just in case… But if he did stumble over a five-star hotel he knew where he would sleep.

Going to the inland side of the beach, against the encroaching forest, and hill, he saw the trees had a wide overhang. He hoped that these would give protection from any breeze and dew. The sand would be soft to sleep on. He hollowed out a shallow bed for himself and even fashioned a sand pillow. From the bush he collected grass to line the hollow with. This would help to hold warmth. He learnt this trick when a boy scout.

After relieving himself and having a swig of water from his bottle, he lay in his sand-bed. It was warm and comfy. Lying on his back, he could see stars speckling through the branches above him. There must have been a breeze as the stars kept disappearing and returning as the branches swayed. He was happy to let his mind wander, it settled on his scouting days. He marvelled at the difference between his youthful innocence and enthusiasm, and his current cynicism. He always loved the bush and the scouting movement. His foster parents would not support him in his interest so he did odd jobs around the neighbourhood to earn the money for the fees and his uniform. How can a life start so brightly, only to tarnish as it did? His mind went to the seagull with the funny leg, wonder what caused the leg to be deformed… perhaps a fish took a bite when the seagull was floating on the ocean. Yet, it seems to have survived okay… nothing is perfect.

He remembered an incident where he was not quite so innocent. At his first scout jamboree, he was the youngest there. He had been looking forward to this for months, that was, until he met Wayne Parnell.

Parnell, a patrol leader with another scout group, was five years older than Stevie and at least a third taller. He was tall and thin with a pointy rat-like face. Stevie remembered how Parnell bullied him and made his time at the camp miserable.

One day Stevie was heading to the latrines, but just before arriving spotted Parnell coming out. Keeping his distance, he ducked behind a tree. When Parnell was out of sight, Stevie snuck into the latrine. Inside, he saw a neatly pressed scout hat sitting on the rope-tied wash stand. It had the insignia of the scout group that Parnell belonged to. Assuming that it was Parnell's, he looked around the hessian walls to see if anyone was within. With the coast clear, and a pounding heart, he dropped the hat down the murky hole and shot out of there as fast as possible. He was grateful that no one was coming into the latrine as he made his exit.

That day an address was to be made by the area scout master, 'Shep'. Of course, all scouts had to attend.

Shep was normally a cheerful and fun man – a round smiling face on a body that had eaten too many scones, his equally round wife cooked. But today his face was as grave as if to report a tragedy. His first words were, "I am afraid that I have some despicable news… Someone did the heinous act of dropping Patrol Leader Parnell's hat into the latrine. This person…" At this stage there was a muffled cheer from many in the parade. "Silence!" Shep shouted. "This incident is of the most severe…"

Droning on like this for some time he did his best to use guilt to pressurize the culprit into admitting his deed.

Stevie was terrified, not of admitting what he did to the Scout Master but what Parnell would do to him afterwards. Not prepared to subject himself to reprisal from that bully, he kept quiet.

Once the parade was dismissed, the camp was abuzz. Everyone was talking about the hat and from what Stevie could gather, most were glad. He even heard one boy say, "Pity Parnell wasn't wearing the hat when it went in."

∞

Lying in his sand bed, he had much to think about. He thought of his supposed death and that wacky African. What tribe did he say he was from? … That's right… Bushman. How did I let myself get talked into this? I'll treat it like the army and do as little as possible and get out as soon as I can. And when I do it will be straight to wherever that tunnel heads. No more debt or responsibility. No need to get pissed anymore. Funny, I never really liked getting drunk but it helped me to forget the life-crap... But… what about Mandy? I'll miss her … she makes me feel good. Arrrgh, forget her, she's better off without me. Besides that last incident… Can't think about that… won't think about it… I was right to chase her away.

He remembered their city apartment, some 1400 kilometres from their hometown. He felt guilty about how he did it; buying her that one-way ticket home. Still, it had to be done. Just one mistake. He should have presented it on the day of her departure, and not the week before. That week sure was long and sad, every night, tears and wailing. Yeah, just forget about her… and now I need to find a way to get out of this place…

∞

What's rustling in the bush? Whatever it was it awoke him. He listened to the night noises, there were many. But there was one that was loud… Seems to be getting closer.

There it is again, even closer.

It was a dark night with thick clouds blocking out any moon light. Peering into the dark, he made out a blob of grey, like a dust-twister.

"Thought you could escape us, didn't you?" This was followed by a shrill laugh. "We are always with you, you know that."

Stevie panicked, "Who are you, and... and... what do you mean? ... Weishka, is that you? This is not funny?

Stevie knew this was not Weishka.

The grey blob was big and close, he could hear its breath. It emitted a revolting smell. Stevie recoiled into the sand in an effort to put space between him and it.

More high-pitched laughing sent shivers through Stevie. "No sense running, Stevie, you can't get away from us."

"Who are you?"

"We are your fears, Stevie. We rule you."

"My fears, what do you mean?"

"We are your friends. After all, you would not let us live in you if you did not allow us. This was followed by more laughing."

Stevie sensed several voices and felt he was going mad. Frantically his hands went to his ears to try to block the thoughts.

"You allowed us to come to you when you were little. It was not long after the demise of the cat." More laughter. "We helped you Steven. We have an agreement."

"What cat are you talking about?"

"Look, we'll remind you."

He was shown a time when he was thirteen. He found a stray kitten in the gutter. It was tiny, about four weeks old. It was jaguar black with not a speck of other color, and so he called it Jet. He instantly loved it and kept it hidden from Joe. Joe didn't like cats.

But two weeks later Joe found Jet. After a lecture on the evils of cats, he grabbed Jet and told Stevie, "Come."

He drove Stevie and Kitty to the local rubbish dump, some five or six kilometers away, and ditched Jet. Then rubbing his hands together in a manner of – now that was easy enough, said, "No more cat." Stevie was devastated as they drove away, leaving a forlorn kitty on top of a pile of old boxes.

The story did not end there as about ten days later, Jet, like a homing pigeon, somehow found its way back. This was miraculous and defied logic, yet there he was. Stevie didn't even have time to fatten him up, when again Jet was discovered by Joe. Rolling up his sleeves, he said, "This time I'll do the job properly." He got a cloth bag out of the shed and put a brick it. Then a meowing and spitting Kitty was shoved into the bag. Joe tied the top of the bag closed with a nylon twine. Stevie was told, "Stay here," as he and the bag drove towards the beach. Upon his return, with a beer in hand, Joe told Stevie with glee that he had thrown the bag with the brick and the cat into the ocean.

Poor Jet, even he could not Houdini his way out of that one. Stevie sobbed into his sand pillow as he remembered the frantic meowing of Jet in the bag. It took a long time before he would speak to Joe again.

For months, after heavy drinking, Joe and Doris kept teasing Stevie with things like, "What's that noise, is it the phantom cat come back again?" While they laughed, Stevie cried inside. He would grit his teeth and not let them see his sadness. He hated them and wished that they would be run over by a bus.

The demon continued and bought Stevie back to the present, "Yes, that cat, now you remember, and so we have an agreement, remember?"

"What agreement?"

"It's easy," said one of the voices, you allow us to live in you and we take care of your self-esteem, and for all of these years this has worked just fine.

Stevie asked, "How do you take care of my self-esteem?"

"We took it away so you don't have any. No self-esteem, no fuss, we are in complete control. We send you messages, just like we are doing now … messages of inadequacy, rage, resentment, and childish tantrums to hide the fact that you have no self-esteem. You remained angry and full of hate… Always the anger. It works very well, especially in your case with your childish tantrums. You don't have to worry about achieving goals or silly things like challenging yourself to get ahead."

"Rubbish, I would never allow this to happen."

"Steven, don't talk nonsense. You know as well as we do that the deal was that you hand over your power to us, and up until now you have been a good and meek boy."

"If I have been a good boy as you say, why did you come to me now?"

"So, you know you are not going to get rid of us so easily. We are your fear and we are here to stay. Don't think just because you are doing this 'journey' that we are leaving. No, ... you can't get rid of us."

Stevie tried again, "I wouldn't have let you stay in me if I knew you were there."

"You, and just about the rest of humanity have no choice. You also know the feelings that we send as a constant reminder of our dominion."

"What feelings?"

"Animosity, anxiety, shame… and the best is self-contempt. When you are confronted with any issues that need a decision, we send timid emotions, such as doom and gloom, the feelings that you call butterflies in your stomach, we increase your heart rate and make you sweat… you know, all the normal fear things."

Finally, it moved away.

Stevie realized that all he had heard was true. He had given his power to his fears. He could see that he had been living to his fears, not allowing his potential to come through. The thought depressed him. The question that Weishka asked when they met was true, "You doubt yourself, don't you?" He did doubt himself, and also doubted support from any source, including what Weishka calls 'The Intelligence'.

He realised, that right now, in this sad state how insidious fear is. I have these feelings and don't even notice. I need to be able to change this and be more positive – at all times.

It was then that he heard Weishka voice, "So often are we conditioned… Listen to this story".

"In the land of Zelta, there was a tribe that lived in the desert regions. For living memory, they had no rain, and forgot what rain was."

"Where the hell is Zelta?" interrupted Stevie.

"Shoosh, just listen."

Chastised, Stevie lent back in his sand hole and with a gesture of grand elegance, indicated the story to continue.

"Although a difficult existence, they were content just to survive and have each other. Drinking water was collected from the sleepy snake-like river that was fed by the far-off mountains. It was a pleasant life, with a silver sun in the deep blue sky.

A day came when far away, on an unknown seaboard, clouds gathered. At first only a few, but like villagers coming to a gathering, they became many until the sky was dark. Rising from the sea they were blown far inland…"

"Jeeze, Weishka, you're a great story teller. Such poetic turn of phrase".

Weishka gave Stevie such a dirty look that Stevie thought better of interrupting again.

"On this particular morning Ferro rose and set out for his day's foraging. He greeted the villagers with a pleasant laugh, and a "How do you do?" He and his friends headed off towards the hills where food was still to be found. They could not understand why it was getting harder to find the succulent roots and bulbs from which they survived.

Later, when Ferro and his friends straightened up to stretch their stiff back's and take a breather, there, with a sharp intake of breath, all exclaiming at the same time, "What's that?" They were looking towards the horizon and saw a dark line that seemed like a fat, dark lizard that stretched across the land. "What an odd thing", they all agreed and sat and watched it for a time. It got bigger, gradually sneaking closer, and as it did, the mood became solemn. "I wonder if this is as the prophet told, the end of all things?" said one.

And as it grew, massive blue-purple thunderheads hovered over them, like angry Gods soon to swoop in and crush them. They swirled menacingly, whilst racing across the sky to devour, and as they did, day became night. Dropping their implements, the men ran towards the village, and their loved ones. As they arrived, panic was everywhere. People shouted, "'It's the end of the world... It's the end of the world'". Frantic mothers hurried to protect their children.

It was at this time, when the angry, blue-purple Gods cracked their anger with a jagged light that blinded eyes, and assaulted the ears. The skin tingled, as if covered in ants. "'To the cave,'" they yelled, "'quickly'" but most of the yelling was lost to the wind.

To their horror, the boulders grabbed the snake-river and pulled it into the sky – then with wrath, hurled the water onto the frightened villagers.

The rain came in sheets, so thick that they could not see five paces in front of them. "'The river... we are in the river... ...quickly, into the cave'". They went deep into the cave hoping to hide, but the howling wind followed, bringing the snake-river with it.

For hours the villagers cowered while the Gods huffed their anger. But finally, after a time, the boulders tired and relented, the wind stilled, and the river put back where it belonged.

They awoke to a normal sunny day, the fierceness gone to terrorize others. Slowly, they left the cave, in one's and two's, only to see the damage to the land... trees lay on their sides, and their huts scattered across the land.

The next day, still shocked, they went out to forage. To their delight they saw green shoots emerging from the land, that would mean the bulbs would grow and become abundant. "'How?'" they wondered.

Stevie, there are times in our life when we look at what we consider to be 'negatives'. But, for every negative there is a corresponding positive. Look for the positive in all instances. It is in recognizing your fear that opens you to growth. You can let your fear go. But to do so you must trust as I learnt to.

∞

Closing his eyes to sleep, he saw what looked like a stick turning lengthways, like a drum majorette's baton flung skywards. He noticed that the stick was crooked. He felt compelled to follow it. High up in the sky and across the land it went. Descending, it fell to the ground unnoticed amongst some children. They were standing on a large rock and were laughing and chatting. One boy, who was larger and older said, "Come Weishka, you can do it, we are all afraid when we start."

Stevie looked at the little boy Weishka. The smile was there but so was an innocence. He must have only been about seven, with bright eyes that shone in the sallow skin. He seemed to huddle within himself.

"Go on," another boy said.

Little Weishka looked over the edge of the cliff. Far below was the rocky ground. Unable to answer he shook his head, "No". He knew that all the other children were watching him and so lowered his eyes. The same boy who had just spoken continued, "Look Weishka, I will do it again," and with this he turned his back to the edge, closed his eyes, and slowly walked backwards to the edge. He did not waver in his slow backward movement, nor did he try to test for the edge with his backwards steps. Just as it seemed that he would topple over, the elder child shouted, "Stop!" Whilst two other children grabbed his arms and pulled him to safety.

Another boy had a turn and when securely away from the edge said, "Weishka, if I can do it so can you."

Weishka's hands were shaking so much he clasped them behind his back. So were his knees, but with determination, and without a word, he turned his back to the edge and closed his eyes. Two boys took his hands and lead him further away from the edge so he would not know how many steps were required. They let his hands go. He stood still, as if stuck to the rock, but after a time took his first faltering step backwards. A cheer went up from the onlookers, then complete silence. Another step, a third and a fourth. There was not a sound. Each successive step seemed a bit more determined than the previous.

Stevie could see into little Weishka's mind, it cried, "Stop, run away!" But he didn't. The fifth and sixth steps took him closer to the edge. His heart pounded with the sound of a thousand wildebeest.

Steps seven and eight became faster as Weishka willed it to end. With half a step to go, Weishka's ninth step went beyond rock and just as he started to fall, the word "Grab!" shattered the stillness. Waiting hands grabbed Weishka's arms and hauled him to safety. Cheers rang across the landscape and could be heard in the village far below. The elders knew another child had found his courage. Weishka stood still and gave a simple smile of satisfaction – his eyes even brighter.

∞

Stevie woke the next morning to the sound of gently breaking waves. Birds sang their way through their foraging, a perfect morning. As he opened his eyes, he saw the thick green forest of the hill he slept under. The gentleness of it was a far cry from the horror of the night before. He could smell the rotting thing that called itself his fears. He remembered the lessons from the story and also the scene with the children and how they beat fear. He said aloud, "I owe you one Weishka."

He also remembered his fear of not wanting to go back to his body before he found himself on the beach. He knew that he did not go back to his body not because of the crap life. He did not go back because of the fear he always felt.

Looking skyward, and at the early sun, he would make the most of this stunning morning and swim. And yes, more oysters and mussels.

Three hours later he was ready to head off, and although he thought the journey of learning a waste of time, he embraced the idea of the hike and was looking forward to pushing his body. There had been many years and much alcohol since his last hike. He longed for the fitness of days past and the power to be able to bound up hills and climb cliff faces. Of late, he had become soft and flabby, and it annoyed him. He made a pact with himself that he would hike at least eight hours a day.

Yesterday, he asked the old man which direction he should hike.

"Whichever you like. It's your hike, and the teachings will find you wherever you are. That you can be sure of."

Standing at the edge of the beach he made his decision. I will go inland and head north, as best as the terrain allows. It may be a bit of a zigzag, but what the hell…

∞

Before heading off he went back to the stream to top up his bottle. On the other side there were reeds with many birds darting in and around, catching tiny flying insects. Whilst sitting there, his eyes were drawn to reeds and he wondered if he could fashion a hat and bag from these.

An hour later he had platted a hat with a wide brim. At first it was difficult getting it to fit his head but with trial and error it worked out just fine. And now for a bag, I need a way to carry all the food that is being sent my way. He first shaped a round wall and then a flat base, which he sewed together to make a basket. Next, he plaited a length of rope, that when attached would enable the basket to hang from his shoulder down to waist height.

He was pleased with the result and enjoyed the time focusing on the projects. Better than purchased items he thought.

∞

To get off the beach and head to the hinterland, there was only one way, and that was up – steep up, and so taking a deep breath he headed towards the hill, hoping to find a track. Soon he did, one that was probably formed by small animals.

The going was tough but it felt good to be hiking. He enjoyed being in nature, the fresh air, exercise, and the freedom of a mind that was not occupied with the wrong thoughts. There is something about effort and nature that invigorates.

It must have taken about two hours to get to the top. Feeling that he had earned a rest, he sat down against a tree, facing the way he had come. He could see the beach and marvelled, I was in that surf not that long ago. He looked far out to sea and could see the slight curve of the horizon. Wonder where that goes in this land on fantasy.

It is like he had walked into a beautiful painting, which was alive on the inside. His mind quickly left the ocean and returned to his predicament. He had difficulty balancing the fact that he was here but not in the physical sense. Yet here he was, in this beautiful coastal bush hiking.

Is it real?

Perhaps I need to see my body again, and with that thought, he was back floating in the ward. It took him a few seconds to adjust to the artificial lighting of the ward, the sounds of instrumentation, and those horrible green walls. There were three different instruments, all flashing different colours. One gave readings of his heart rate, oxygen uptake, and more that Stevie could not understand. The other two fed stuff into his body by inserted lines. One started beeping, and the words flashed "Finished". A young nurse, a trainee, carried a bedpan to a grumpy old man, "Hurry up nurse, I'll piss myself…"

Stevie looked at his own face on the bed. It was pasty, without expression or colour, his eyes eerily open, lifeless – the blinkless stare of a doll. His head was covered in wires that connected to a monitor. Even the graphs on the monitor looked lifeless. Just a flat beep, every so often.

How could life lead me to this point? It was not long before his mind went back to the horrors of the orphanage… and then his foster parents. He was eight and remembered his excitement at their pending arrival. The head orderly told him, "Stay clean as the man and lady are coming to get you and I don't want them to not take you because you are a grubby little thing. Do you hear me?"

Stevie saw himself make an exaggerated nod with shyness. Big eyes looking up at the orderly.

It seemed he had waited in that room for hours. The stone floor was black with white squares. Every time someone came into the room he looked up in hope. He felt scared and uncertain. The morning turned to afternoon, then late afternoon. Finally, they came. He was big, with a beard and fat stomach. She was small, skinny and spoke with a loud nasal screech. "Come on," she said, "we don ave all day. We gotta get back home."

That was the day that he started to hate life…

∞

Returning to his place under the tree he felt that somehow, he needed to try and come to terms with his situation. Like the seagull with the dodgy leg. He thought that he would try a meditation. Perhaps if he could learn to control his mind, he may be able to control the fears that came to him, and come to terms with how he treated his son. But, never having meditated before he did not know how to go about it. He closed his eyes and tried to focus on his mind, or what he thought was his mind. This seemed to be the place where thoughts came from but he was not sure. He tried to still his mind, to slow the thoughts down, but they just kept coming, thought after thought. Every so often there was a space of nothingness. However, as soon as he recognised this nothingness he was back in his normal thought-swamped consciousness.

Patience had never been one of Stevie's strong points and he soon got frustrated, until he received the gentle words from Weishka, "It's okay… we all learn sometime. Can I help you?"

"Yeah, not doing too well on my own. This nothingness is like wet soap won't be hung on to."

"Good," whispered Weishka. "I want you to continue with your eyes closed but mentally observe yourself and your surroundings."

Stevie felt his backside on the ground, his back against the tree, with the bark unevenly pressing into his spine. He felt a whisper of breeze on his face and heard the distant surf. A fly or insect buzzed, and the branches of the tree waved in the breeze…

"Now, you need to relax your body. Starting from the top of your head, work down, softening each body part. As you do this, be aware of your breathing becoming deeper but gentler. Do all of this in your own time."

As Stevie did, Weishka watched and felt the process. When Stevie had finished, he said, "Now that you are feeling more relaxed. Listen to the sounds around you. Don't think about them, just be with them."

Stevie could feel himself slide deeper into himself, and as he did, he became aware of the absolute silence of his mind. At first it was oppressive. He realized that this was the first time in his life he had allowed his mind to focus on nothing, other than the thoughts that swam across his consciousness. This was very different from his worries and the perpetual need for his mind to be active and amused. The silence was scary and uncomfortable. Stay with it, you can handle this, he thought.

At first it was difficult but after a time his mind and body fused into one and the noisy-silence diminished. Like a cat watching a lizard, he watched the thoughts crawl across his mind. Some seemed to come and go, others clung with a tenacity that demanded attention. These were the thoughts that challenged him. Most wanted to reduce his power and were negative and reminded him of past issues. There was a time he found his mind strayed and he was thinking about those fear-things that assaulted him last night.

Stevie did not want to be confronted with this challenge. Weishka had said to him to use meditation to examine past events, especially events that had a strong influence. Stevie was smart enough to know that the confronting would be a confrontation with his very being. He was scared and would prefer that it all went away. But he knew it wouldn't and that there was a part of him that would nag until it had its way. The current subliminal playback was at the orphanage. No one told him why he lived in an orphanage. And, if he had a mum or dad, he knew nothing about them but whoever they were, they didn't want him… Why was I not wanted? Joe and Doris said I am bad… The people in the orphanage said I was bad…

He remembered bath-time in the orphanage. There were two bathrooms adjacent to each other. These were small cubicles that contained the bath. If they had doors they were never closed. The children approached the bathroom from two queues, one for girls, and the other for boys. In each bath there was only one lot of water for all those in the queue, and so the kids at the back could almost stand on the water. Stevie chuckled at the remembrance.

The production line moved in a steady progression, and at regular intervals all took a step closer to the bath.

There were two orderlies per bathroom. As a child reached the door, one orderly stripped him or her naked. That happened in conjunction with another kid being washed in the bath. When this infant was deemed to be cleaner than when he started, he would be prodded to step out of the bath and the next child would step in. Each had to squat, whilst the second orderly ran a flannel over them as if to scour the dirt off. In no time the child was out of the bath, dried and dressed.

On this day, Stevie saw himself in the queue, towards the back and was doing what all normal boys do – that is talk and have fun. This did not suit the undressing orderly who told him to keep quiet. He did for a minute or two but forgot and started chirping again. The angry orderly thundered towards him and roughly grabbed his ear and dragged him into the middle of the girls' queue and told him, "You bath with them."

Stevie knew nothing about girls. They were alien, and he felt that he had been delivered into the hands of a strange species. Being acutely aware of his difference, he tried to cover himself. He was mortified and wanted to disappear under that muddy water and never re-surface. The girls were equally embarrassed.

E M E R G E N C Y   R O O M …
S U N D A Y   5 : 5 2   A M

Rose waited for Doctor Ritchie. He said that he would come and check the patient before finishing his shift at 6:00 am, "If there is no improvement by then I'll conduct brain tests and have him declared brain dead and turn off the ventilator."

Rose knew what this meant.

∞

Coming out of the meditation Stevie was still disturbed with the images of the orphanage and so headed off straight away, pushing his body to the limit, as if to purge himself. He worked his legs hard and pumped his arms in an effort to go as fast as he could. So determined, his surroundings went unnoticed and swept past in an angry daze. He thought, *Even as a child I knew that the adults in my young life, and in the orphanage, had failed me… I always felt I would never fail any child of mine – but I did – bigtime!*

But towards the end of the morning he started to gain better perspective and calmed down. Reflecting on this, he realized that his furious behaviour to purge something within was a lifelong habit. This realization was a good one and he made a mental note to try and recognize its next occurrence.

Later, with a drifting mind, again he thought of the scout-hat incident. This bought a smile to his lips. *Wonder what Weishka would think about what I did?*

No sooner he thought that, he heard, "Nothing is hidden."

"Do you always listen to my thoughts? Have I no privacy."

There was no reply from Weishka.

"Well, was it bad what I did?"

"We don't make judgements."

"Would you have done it, if you came in and saw the bully's hat there?"

"We all do what we have to do," was the reply, with a slight hint of mirth.

E M E R G E N C Y   R O O M …
S U N D A Y   6 : 0 2   A M

Mandy had flown in and took a cab directly from the airport to the hospital.

∞

As Rose was doing her rounds and walking past the nurse's desk, she heard the name Steven Jardine. Looking at the source of the voice she saw a young woman leaning over the desk. Joanna, a young nurse said, "Steven Jardine is four beds down on the right."

With that, the lady went towards Steven's bed. Rose continued her work but could not help wonder who the visitor was. *Shame… she looks sad.*

∞

The thick canopy made the track gloomy, but patches of sunlight gave shape to the deep shade. Moss covered trees and rocks added to the gloom. As he walked leaves crunched underfoot.

It took about two hours to work his way down a ravine. He found a stream and quenched his thirst with the soft nectar. As he filled his water bottle his mind worked. The old man was right when he said I have a million questions. He thought of the funny description of the cluttered child's room. I have always been like this. He remembered the start of one school year, the form teacher said in exasperation, "But Steven, you cannot do nineteen extracurricular activities!"

Sitting, he watched the stream and loved how the sunlight flickered broken silver flashes, here there, gone now. Insects skimmed across the surface of the water in a never-ending search for food. Was it a dance or a chore? Small waterfalls fed a bubbling sound, a leaf floated past, heading to who knows where.

Questions such as; if positive thinking works, as the old man had suggested, then what hidden force makes it so? It was not long before he had the answer. "You create for tomorrow what you are today. And so, if you are without fear now, the next day will be better."

Further contemplating the value of this 'journey', the thought came to his mind, unless, and until man embarks on this quest of the true self, doubt and uncertainty will follow his footsteps through life.

Hell, where did this come from? But before he had much time to think about it, he felt himself spontaneously relaxing, much the same as when he did the meditation earlier. From there his mind drifted… seeing himself, as if in a dream … …It seemed that he was born into darkness, where images could just be discerned. Roots of trees as thick as a man's body lay strewn above the ground, like slumbering serpents supporting trunks of massive height and girth. Thick humus carpeted the ground, debris from the solid canopy that hid the sky far above. It was soft to walk on, damp and mossy. The grotto of his mind was a cold and thriving place for all manner of creepy-crawly things, things that slithered in the near dark. Leaves constantly rustled as some creature scurried away from a predator, or was the predator. Things growled and hissed as combatants struggled for survival.

In this cauldron of his early life, fear clutched at his gut and was a constant companion. He knew this feeling. He knew that to stay in this claustrophobic dungeon was to be vulnerable. Was this the earth plane that he wanted to leave? He had endured this tomb of mind from childhood to adulthood. But now a sense niggled at his mind, pushing him to move and seek something better. He did not know where this sense came from, but felt it could be trusted. Determined to leave the relative security of the known for the unknown, and set off to find himself. Is this dream prophetic of his past life, and now this journey?

At first his progress was slow, and for a time it seemed to get even darker, which scared him more. But as he grew and developed, he learnt that to move from one mind space to another can incur darkness, as our fear takes over. He continued the journey, his journey of learning, stumbling on, falling over life's impediments and overcoming difficulties. For this journey of self, he was alone. He had to be, as no one could share it with him. Nor did he have any idea of the direction to take – how could he? He did not know the destination, and if he did, how could he know if he had made it? Never having faced himself before it felt awkward, like wearing a coat backwards.

He wondered if this was a dream or part of this journey of learning. Either way, it was hard but he continued.

It was difficult cutting through the thick bush that clung to him, a thousand silent arms – arms like beggars searching, restraining and clutching, demanding. The path was always uphill. His arms and legs were exhausted from the pushing and pulling as he climbed higher and higher. At times he would slip and plummet to a point where he had been some time before. He would lie there feeling sorry for himself and wonder what lesson he was supposed to learn. It crossed his mind many times to give up, as the journey was too arduous. Nevertheless, he struggled on.

After a while he started to learn the ways of his inner realm and it became easier. He developed an assurance that things would keep improving, and so he was able to cover more ground. The once formidable dark and dank depths of his inner self did not seem so hostile. It was the same, yet different. What had changed? He had, and as if to support his evolution, he was given beams of light that radiated through the bush, showing the way. It illuminated the jungle of his mind, giving beauty and form to its interior. But there was more journeying to be done, and so onwards and upwards he clambered.

Once he came face to face with glowing eyes, from a menacing long black shape. It snarled and spat, while its breath soured his nostrils. Had this creature confronted him earlier, it would have devoured him, but he held his nerve and it slunk away.

Although it seemed to be years that he had been on this journey, he sensed that he was making progress, as the darkness gradually gave way to light. High above, through the trees, was blue. He could not understand what this was, but felt it to be friendly. As he continued, somehow, he knew that his direction was correct and that each step took him assuredly to a warmer and lighter place.

Suddenly, he was out of the jungle and on a stone ledge that jutted out of the valley wall. The sun shone a golden protection, nurturing and comforting. The open space liberating.

He looked over the jungle that had previously owned him and could see the rivers that he forded and the scrub that had cut his hands. At the time he could not see any logic or plan to it, but now it was all so obvious and perfect. From his position of elevation, the wilds were beautiful. Yet to reach this point he had been obliged to travel through those wilds and endure the experiences.

Gradually the trance wore off, and Stevie was left to ponder, the words that he had been given, 'Unless, and until man embarks on this quest of the true self, doubt and uncertainty will follow his footsteps through life.'

Well, that makes sense he thought, especially with the vision that he journeyed through. The vision he just had must be an analogy of this etheric journey. Well, I hope its message of coming out of the dark into the light happens. Feeling a pain, he looked at his hand, and there he saw a cut, and he remembered how one of the vines in the trance had broken his skin… what the hell?

After resting, he felt stronger, forged in the knowledge of who he could be, and that perhaps, just perhaps, this journey of learning may help him.

∞

Night had fallen. He had eaten the last of the seafood he picked for the day but was able to supplement it with wild berries he found. They were sour and he hoped they would not make him sick.

Climbing into his new burrow for the night, he was anxious that he would not have a repeat visit from his fear. After the day's exertion, he soon fell asleep.

∞

A few days later, and on a hot and advanced morning, Stevie looked for a place to rest. He had been following a valley. Halfway down, he found a wild banana tree. The bananas were small and irregularly shaped but were the tastiest he had eaten. Probably because they were not grown with all the chemicals they pump into the ground these days. He picked as many as he could carry, loading his pockets, a couple under his hat, and packed his bag – a walking banana tree.

As he got farther down the valley, he could tell from a clump of trees that there was a stream. He had been going through thick overgrowth and suddenly emerged into bright sunlight. There in front of him was a pool of water about thirty metres long. The water was brown from the tannins of the surrounding vegetation. It looked cool and inviting.

He stood on a rock that over looked the water and took off his clothes. Luxuriating with the sun on his back he rested for a while. Whilst eating a banana, he examined the surroundings. He always loved the freedom of being out in the open without clothes, and of course skinny-dipping is the best way to swim. The walking had been good for him. Already his skin was turning a golden brown from the sun and he felt his body firming up. He was feeling good about himself. Certainly, that vision of the emerging from the valley helped. He realised that he had been off all substances since he had been here, and was pleased to realise that he had not thought of them for a few days. Goes to show you that a different mind-set does produce a different result. He wondered if that vision was about him emerging from the dark to the light, was emerging from the cloaking of the substances he had taken for the last few years – that the dark damp jungle, with a thousand silent arms that clutched and restrained, reflected his substance abused mind.

Being careful not to slide on the algae he worked his way into the water. When about thigh-height, he dived in and swam underwater for a few strokes. Not cold at all, he thought. He swam to express his energy, and every so often swam under water. It was deep, and the deeper he went, the colder the water. Slowing it down, and relaxing, he lay on his back and floated and looked up at the deep blue sky and the overhanging trees that surrounded the pond. Every so often a bird flew in and out of his vision. After a time, he went to sit in the sand to warm up in the sun.

Relaxed and happy, his mind turned to the things that he had learnt since meeting Weishka. He called him now, "Weishka, come in Weishka", as if calling on a two-way radio.

"I'm here."

"Weishka, how does it work that when we think positive thoughts that positive situations are more likely to occur?"

"Well, I could tell you, but it would be best to show you. Let's go back a few minutes before you swam. You felt good."

Stevie was able to watch the scene. He saw himself sitting on the rock in the sun and taking off his clothes.

Weishka said, "Stare at your body, try not to blink, and tell me what you see."

Doing so, and after a moment, Stevie could see a light sheen around his body. "What is it?"

Weishka said, "Keep staring and colour will emerge as you get used to it. Everything is a vibration – the bricks in a wall, steel, the trees, everything. There is nothing on Earth that does not vibrate with life. You humans have instruments that measure vibration. Quantum physics proves that all solids are nothing more than vibration. All creatures emit a consistent range of frequencies – in general; the more primitive the organism the lower the vibration.

In time Stevie was able to see color. It was swirling, like oil trapped in water when light shines on it. The vibrant colors were iridescent and brighter than any he had experienced. The predominant color was a rich dark blue. The entire effect encircled his body by about two meters.

Continuing, Weishka said, "Advance animals have lower frequencies. For instance, the range that an ant emits is around 1500 KHz. Humans start from about 9000 KHz. For this discussion, what we are interested in is the fact that frequencies can be measured and seen as you are doing now. Each human has his or her own unique frequency. These and the color change according to the mood. That's why music, which is also a vibration, can change our mood. A human, therefore, in a specific mood would emit a specific vibration, or rather, a frequency. Now, let's go and see your energy change when your fear visited you on your first night."

Once again Stevie was a witness to the scene with his fear blob and trained his gaze at his body. He was amazed to see that the color was an insipid lemon color. It only shone about six hundred millimeters from his body.

"You have seen Stevie that as your mindset changes, so does your vibrational frequency. The higher the frequency the more etheric or immaterial the being is. I for instance, vibrate at a much higher frequency than you. I could have started this teaching by saying everything is energy as it is energy that produces vibration. For now, I want to show you one more example."

Stevie was back at the rock with the Bushman children and was told to look at little Weishka's energy. He did and saw that it was a weak light blue that only emanated about two hundred millimetres from his body. But as little Weishka started to walk backwards and claimed his power, the colour changed to a strong maroon and green that billowed far from his body.

Weishka spoke again, "There is another thing that you need to understand, and that is that vibration does not suggest a class system. Everything in the universe is of value. A low vibration does not mean that that the vibrating thing is of lower worth. Humans have developed a camera that takes photos of auras. This is called Kirlian Photography."

Stevie jumped in with a thought, "Can I see these various energy forms as well?"

"Yes, with practice but to see these things you must raise your vibration. When your vibration is low, as you have seen, your power is reduced."

"How do I do that?" Stevie asked.

"This is not as difficult to do as you would think but it does take dedication. Without knowing it, you change your vibration all the time, depending on your mood so the calmer the mind the faster the vibration... or, the more negative a mind-set, the lower the vibration. Stevie, why do you think the yogis and so-called mystics strive to become yogis and mystics?" Weishka answered his own question, "To raise their vibration, and by doing so they are able to visit more non-material aspects.

Let me give you an example. A car is fuelled by petrol. Your spiritual growth is fuelled by your thoughts. If the petrol that is put in the car is inferior then the car will progressively deteriorate. If your mind fuels itself with inferior thoughts, your life will progressively malfunction and you will move farther away from the right vibration."

Stevie was silent as if making up his mind and then said in a determined way, "I see what you have shown me, but I have no intention of becoming a yogi, a mystic or anything else that requires me to go back to my body. I ended it because of the crap." Then, in a softer voice, "No... I can't go back."

"Cross, cross, cross. Why so cross? No one is forcing you to do anything that you don't want to do. If you want to end your journey of learning you can any time you want. On Earth and beyond Earth, everything you do is a choice. It is your choice to be cross. It is also your choice to continue with me." Weishka said no more and let the silence do its work.

Stevie felt the heavy silence and did not like its challenging taunt. Trying to ignore it, he kept doodling. At one stage he snuck a glance at Weishka, whose smile broadened even more, accentuating his high cheek bones. Realising that he could not fill the silence he gruffly said, "While I am here, I might as well continue, but only for a while. But when I'm ready I will end all of this. Do you understand?"

Weishka proceeded as if nothing had happened, "Now look at your vibration... this angry one". Stevie did, and was shocked to see it was weak in colour and nearly flat against his body.

Weishka was quiet as Stevie took this in. Then he continued, "Just a thought for you… When I was quiet, and you squirmed whilst I waited for you to say your piece… Stevie, silence is your friend. Don't avoid it, embrace it. It is in silence that you reach beyond yourself. Energy is a creative force. If the universe and everything within it is energy then it is reasonable to accept that it was energy that formed the universe. This means that energy is a creative force. How does that sound?"

With more enthusiasm he said, "And so God… or the Intelligence, is energy, creative energy. Is that correct?"

With equal excitement, Weishka said, "In principle, yes, but remember I said earlier that there are various forms of energy. As your Einstein said, energy never dissipates – it merely changes form. What you refer to as God is the purest energy."

"Weishka, now that I have seen it, I can believe this. Tell me more about the positive thinking."

Weishka went on, "As you are energy, you also are a creator, you create with your thoughts. Now the energy, or lack of it, as you saw around yourself, is determined by your positive or negative mind. It is what determines your creative ability."

Stevie nodded his head several times.

Weishka continued, "Thoughts are energy, or to put it another way, they are directed energy." Then, slowing down for emphasis, "It means that every thought that you have is potential creation. And the more thoughts that you have on an issue the more power you give it."

Stevie gulped as if he had physically swallowed the ideas and asked, "So am I the sum total of all my thoughts?"

"Indeed, you are. To get to the point of wanting to end your life because of your difficulties, your predominant thought process was one of being more negative than positive… You've not needed substances here because you have been more positive… Well generally… you still have little out bursts, like the one a few minutes ago… but generally you are more positive."

"I guess so."

"I want you to absorb what I have shown you so will finish by saying, just as you are the result of your collective thoughts, humanity's situation is also the result of their combined thoughts. Energy does not direct itself, it is propelled from the direction given it. It does not care. It is like a genie from a bottle that will grant you any wish, irrespective of it being good for you or not. So, for the things you want in life you must propel the energy in the right way."

EMERGENCY ROOM ...
SUNDAY 6:15 AM

At 6.15 Ritchie arrived. He had replaced his green hospital scrubs with casual clothes and a smart suede jacket. Rose could see that he was on his way out.

She hovered impatiently as he checked the chart and instrumentation and could not keep still.

"Did the lab return to tell us what was ingested?"

"Yes and no," said Rose. "He did drink a large quantity of whiskey, but so far they have not traced the other substance or substances."

"Yeah, so the paramedic said." And then more to himself, and with a distinct sigh, "Probably won't make much difference at this stage anyway." And then louder to Rose, "What about the lung inflammation results?"

"The lab is short staffed. Apparently two staff members are down with a virus. They said they will try and have the results a bit later this morning... But there is something more, his Glasgow Coma rating is now down to two".

"Rose, get the paperwork ready to request a supporting diagnosis from neurology. There is nothing more that we can do. Also see if you can get hold of a relative for permission for organ donorship."

Rose knew that his manner of instruction was to hide the sadness and futility of this life lost.

Reaching out her hand, she touched his arm, "Can't we leave him on support a bit longer…please?"

Ritchie looked at his head nurse. They had worked together for many years, he knew her well. He also knew that she had lost her only son William in a car accident a while back. The patient was about William's age.

Knowing there were no other emergency cases, said, "Okay, Rose, let the next shift take the responsibility."

∞

With morbid fascination Stevie watched his body. For the first time he noticed that there was some sort of pump on his heart to keep it beating. He was in a ward with curtains around three sides of his bed. There was no one in the area, just his body. A machine biped at regular intervals. The area was gloomy and instrument lights illuminated it in a soft red glow, whilst the screen flickered shadows on the walls. Quickly scanning his energy field, he saw that it was flat to his body and grey in colour.

For what seemed like hours, Stevie just stared at his body and still had difficulty with the concept that he could see it, yet he was surreally separate from it. Much of the time his mind was blank, at other times he thought of the events of his life. Seeing the image of his heart on the screen made him think of how often in life his heart seemed to beat anger and not blood. It was anger that pumped and circulated through his body, the heart its epicentre. Being separated from his body as well as the normal issues of his life, he was able to see and understand with clarity. He was grateful that Weishka often kept away at these times, as if to give Stevie the space to process.

He did not know how long he hovered there, but saw the interaction between the nurse and the doctor and thought of the consequences of not returning to his body. The old man said that I would have to return in another life to complete what I need to learn. Damn, why do I have to take responsibility for this…?

∞

Late that afternoon, after preparing his burrow he took off his shoes. These were the running shoes he had on when he committed suicide. He had done a lot of walking since then and wanted to inspect them. Thinking that they would be starting to disintegrate, he was amazed that there seemed to be no wear or tear. Hmmm, I have a hat, water bottle and so far, plenty of water and food, and now against all expectation my shoes seem to be holding up okay. Perhaps the vision of my coming from the dark to the light may happen… Nah, silly thought.

∞

With an advanced dawn his awareness took hold. Cold and damp from rain, and with seized muscles, it took time to straighten out. A heavy day with more rain to come, he thought. His mood matched the darkness of the clouds. What he wondered last night was forgotten? Yawning and stretching, he thought, I want a hot, strong coffee. An involuntary shiver brought his mind back to the present. He was hungry. The bananas were finished and he had not been able to find more. Let's get this fucking walk over with, he thought, and hobbled off towards the next hill. He could not see how high it was as it was mist-enshrouded.

He walked with a limp, his right calf torn from a fall he had yesterday. At the time it did not feel too bad but now it was swollen and bruised. Feeling sorry for himself he continued moaning. I'm hungry, I want coffee – what am I doing here? This sucks… For a moment he wondered if he was back in his body.

Weishka, he thought, "I want out." No answer. "Weishka, where are you? … Come on old man… don't bugger me around." The only answer was another heavy downpour. The cold stiffened his shoulders and rain trickled down his back with icy fingers.

Without realising it, his mind, and all the negatives, dominated every second – one hundred percent of his consciousness was negative. After a time, he exploded, "That's it… Get me out of here – now! I quit… You win, I lose… I've had enough of these games." Puffing with anger and indignation, he raised a fist as if to threaten something in the sky. His voice broke when he said, "I wish I was dead." For a split second he nearly laughed at the absurdity of the thought, as he was already dead –

well, sort of. But he liked being full of anger – an old friend. Really dead, not like this shit. I'm so tired of battling. Battling is all I do, all I am.

He stopped walking and stood there feeling sorry for himself, his breath heavy. It could have been a minute or ten. The rain made channels in his hair and dropped to his face. An involuntarily shiver shook his body, his teeth chattered.

"Weishka, if this is a test, it's stupid and I refuse to participate."

The shivering continued, like a motor idling. Better keep walking before I freeze to death. The gloomy day crept into a cold cheerless night. His amble was slow, partly because of his misery, partly because of his hunger, and partly because of the rain-black night. He felt like he was walking in a cave without a torch. Many times, he stumbled or fell, adding grazes to his worsening calf muscle.

He looked for somewhere to get out of the rain and to sleep. Tonight, he found no such place. More annoyed, and with growing hunger, he wondered if the first few days of manifesting had been a fluke and that it did not really work.

He heard the thought, "Look at the contents of your mind."

"Weishka, is that you? Are you there?!"

Silence.

Damned wizard, I know it was you, Stevie thought, as he groped his way through featureless black.

What did he say? Stevie thought. He said, "Look at the contents of your mind." What does he mean by that? What the hell is wrong with my mind? There is nothing wrong with it. I'm just a tad angry and frustrated. Who wouldn't be if they were stuck in this hell? … That's it, he thought, I have finally died and have gone to Hell... Yes, Hell, that's where I am.

Hearing childlike laughter, he thought, that dog Weishka is laughing at me…there it is again. This time it was loud enough to be heard over the patter of rain drops. The sod is laughing at me. Why is he laughing at me? Unless, he stopped with the realization,… unless he is the devil!

This time Weishka's laughing was completely out of control, with long breathless guffaws.

Stevie tried to shout his anger but nothing came out other than a frustrated squeak.

As Weishka reined in his run-away mirth he re-planted the words, "Look at the contents of your mind."

"Either get me out of here or leave me alone."

If Stevie hoped to spark an argument or gain sympathy he was mistaken. He continued stumbling on. "Ouch," he moaned, as he walked into a low-hanging branch that scratched his forehead. "I'm freezing, starving to death, exhausted, lonely, it's pitch dark, and he says look at the contents of my mind."

He wandered aimlessly, the rain continued, and so did his shivering. Damn him… What does he mean look at the contents of my mind? Hmmm… my mind? It was then that he realized that the walls of his mind oozed anger. A seething mass of resentment that boiled with victimization. With insight he saw that these thoughts were so dominant he had lost all reason – almost as if his mind had been removed and replaced with something that crawled and hissed. How could my mind be so alien and overpowering? Surely my mind is me, and I am my mind? My fear said something about me running away in anger.

Again, he remembered the vision where … it showed he thought that he was *born into darkness… Roots of trees as thick as a man's body lay strewn above the ground, like slumbering serpents, supporting trunks of massive height and girth… The grotto of his mind was a cold and thriving place for all manner of creepy-crawly things, things that slithered in the near dark. Leaves constantly rustled as some creature scurried away from a predator, or was the predator. Things growled and hissed as combatants struggled for survival…*

He knew the journey that he saw was an allegory of his thought process, as was the coming out into light as he did at the end. If I am my mind and if my mind can turn on me or turn me into a… a raving depressed idiot then what hope is there for me? Thinking further, he realized that he was like this just before he committed suicide, and many times in his life. What was it that Jenny, his last girlfriend, said to him when she was about to dump him, "You surround yourself with negativity." He could see that she was right. This darkened state of mind is pathological. So, if I am my mind, and if my mind is gloomy, then I will also be gloomy.

I wonder what colour my energy field is at the moment, probably black. For as long as I remember my mind had been a traitor to me that robbed me of happiness and optimism. Yet, if I am my mind, then I must be the creator of my thoughts.

Returning to the concepts of the contents of his mind, he reasoned, surely the mind is or should be my servant. Seems to me it is like a TV set that has no channel changer and plays what it wants. Damn it, I must grab the control to play what I want to play, something that is best for me.

Stevie was pleased with the understanding and further realized that in only a few seconds he had swung his mind from separation of non-rationality to rationality. All it took was to look at the contents of his mind. He realized that the rain had stopped and even a star or two twinkled. He wondered if his mind created the storm. Why not, he reasoned? My depressed mind made me depressed and now that my mind reflects harmony, perhaps it created harmony. Testing this he sent out thoughts of warmth. As he did his clothes started to dry and the cold left him. This is amazing, let me try something else, so generated thoughts of well-being. After a time, his shoulders did not seem as stiff and his calf felt better. He chuckled to himself when he remembered his thought that he was in hell and Weishka the devil.

"Yes," interrupted Weishka, "Best laugh for several life-times. But now, Stevie, think back and see how you thought yourself into and out of hell."

He did and asked, "What is this place that creates what my mind thinks?"

Weishka answered, "You are in a different realm that is less dense than Earth and as a result your thoughts manifest faster than on Earth."

Stunned Stevie said, "You mean that even on Earth our minds build a life that resembles what is in the mind?"

"Yes, it does. It is slower on Earth but you really do become the sum total of your thoughts."

The old man was quiet as Stevie remembered the difficult life that he had and how most of the time his mind was irritated. He said, "Now I'm starting to understand what you meant when you said that I had an uncomfortable life because I did not know how to live it."

"That's part of it," agreed Weishka. "But let's talk about the mind for a while. As you saw, you were lost to reality… or rather the moment. What I mean by the moment is what is happening in your mind at any time. The moment is just one frame of all moments that make up all time. Understand?"

Grappling with this concept he hesitated, until finally nodding his head, "I think so."

"Good, then give an example."

"Well, that at all times, second by second, it's imperative I know what's going on in my mind. Is that right? I was pretty much one hundred percent negative. I must be aware, so I can make it as positive as possible."

"Yes," said Weishka whilst silently clapping his hands in applause, "and by knowing the contents of your mind, you can see if it is happy or sad, and if sad, you can change it – like you did now. You will see if it is full of debilitation or inspiration… … in the vision you had of the dark jungle of your mind, you were able to move from a dark mind to a lighter mind. That was just a vision, but its reality is possible. It's up to you.

Stevie interrupted, "You mean positive or negative?"

"Absolutely. I am glad that you understand this point as it is because of mind's full of negativity that most people have difficulty living a good life. But know, many people want to learn and grow. Yet when it happens and things become unfamiliar, they get scared and panic. They try and scurry back to what was familiar. For growth to happen you have to be prepared to change things, sometimes the most basic of things."

They were both quiet for a while until Stevie asked, "Is that why I didn't manifest any food since the other day… or a place to sleep because I was angry, not trusting and not feeling love?"

"That's correct," said his master.

∞

Stevie felt compelled to visit his body again, and like before, once the decision had been made, he was instantly there. Cool being able to do this, he thought. He was amused at being attached to the ceiling as if fastened with Velcro. Bird's-eying the scene he instantly felt a lump of grief in his throat as he saw Mandy sitting next to his body. Seeing her big tear-watered eyes, and the unconscious childlike way she was twisting and untwisting her hair bought tears to his eyes.

"Mandy!" he shouted.

Blankly, she continued the hair twisting.

"Mandy, here I am… can't you hear me?" With all the force his vocal cords could muster he shouted, "Damn… I'm here Mandy"

"I've got to get her to see me." With that thought the Velcro released and he was on the floor next to her. Her distant, sad tear-filled stare continued right through him. She mumbled, "Stevie, my beautiful man, why did you do this?"

For a split-second Stevie thought she was talking to him, the him next to her, not the body on the bed but realized she was talking to herself.

He wanted to hold her and tell her it was okay, and that… He stopped the thought, he just wanted to hold her.

"Perhaps if I was better to you, you may not have sent me away," she said.

"No, no, Mandy, don't say that. It was my fault… I… I was scared to love you… love hurts."

"I thought we were able to work through our differences. When we moved into the flat together, we had so much hope…you were so sweet… well most of the time… not when you had your gloomy periods. You have always been prone to depression. And then out of the blue you just ended it… Perhaps it was the substances that made it worse."

Whimpering louder she said, "I shouldn't have gone. I should have ripped up the ticket. If you live… as the angels are my witness… I will never let you dump me again. But even if you live, you would not want me after what I did to our child. How could you forgive me?" With this, she slumped over the bed and sobbed.

Watching her as he was, out of the blue he remembered with fondness the day that they had arranged to spend together. Keeping it quiet, they did not tell any of their school friends, and hoped that they would not bump into any. It was a Saturday morning, and Stevie had to lie to Joe and tell him that he had an athletics day at another school. Otherwise, Joe would not have let him out of his sight. It seemed that Joe enjoyed keeping Stevie locked in as often as possible. Stevie knew that he was safe with this lie because there was no way either of his foster parents would go anywhere near the school athletic ground. It was the couch, the TV, and alcohol for them.

To facilitate the lie, Stevie got dressed in his athletic clothes, but in his day pack he had placed the clothes that he wanted to wear. He slowly went out the door as if he was in no hurry, but he could hardly contain his excitement. He made sure that he ambled to the corner, and only once around it did his exuberance take over and he ran.

Down the road there was a park with a clean public toilet. It was to this that he headed to change his clothes. He put on his best pair of casual shorts and his brand-new top. Stevie was not often given new clothes but he had been given this top only a week earlier. His foster parents never went to a 'normal' store to buy clothes, they always went to the charity shops and bought from there. On this occasion his foster mother had found a barrel that had brand-new shirts, still in their sealed packages but at almost giveaway prices. So, she bought this one for Stevie. It was a sports shirt with colored vertical stripes of green, red and white. The collar was blue and the shirt was a perfect fit. Stevie was delighted and felt good in it.

He hid his day pack with his athletic clothes in some bushes beside the toilet where he would retrieve them on the way home. He ran the rest of the way to the bus stop where he was to meet Mandy. Although he was five minutes early, she was already there waiting for him. When he arrived, she stood up from the bus stop bench. There was a moment of awkwardness, were it seemed that they wanted to give each other a quick hug but both were too shy. Hiding this, she said, "You're puffing, you've been running?"

"I didn't want to be late", he said as he sat on the bench.

She sat next to him. Neither said anything. It was the first time since they had met as children that there had any awkwardness. She was wearing a pair of jeans and a white T-shirt with a big Mickey Mouse on it. He could not help notice that she had to wear a bra – it never occurred to him that she would ever have to. He felt young and immature in comparison. Although he was thirteen and she was twelve, she was a bit taller than him. He wished that he was able to shave but his face was smooth, with not a hint of a hair.

Sensing his awkwardness, and hers, she thought it silly, and to break the mood she said, "We're going to have such fun. Mum gave me some extra pocket money so we can go on as many rides as we want… and I dare you to come on 'The Thumper'."

"Year, I'll go with you no problem." He said this without knowing what the thumper was. It was then that the bus, number twenty-one came, which took them to the city terminus. From there they caught an outgoing bus, number forty-nine that went to the fairground. The awkwardness had disappeared as they chatted the whole way.

They had half a dozen different rides when Stevie said to Mandy, "I'm hungry. Wanna a hotdog?"

"No way. You sure you want one of those things before you go on 'The Thumper'?"

"Yep, why not?"

Mandy said nothing and just grinned.

Having consumed the hotdog, with traces of tomato sauce on his chin and also on his shirt, she led him to the other side of the grounds. As they got closer, they could hear a loud and intermittent thumping. "What's that?" he asked.

"That's The Thumper", she replied.

And although still some distance away from it, it got louder and louder until Stevie looked up and saw a mammoth arm extending into the sky. It looked a bit like a train carriage that was attached to a vertical rail. It was slowly heading upward with the people firmly strapped in. Stevie could feel their anticipation from where he was. He stopped to watch, as it got to its zenith, it rounded the top, paused for a second before plunging vertically downwards, at what seemed to be G-force speed, as screams filled the air. As it got to the bottom it hit a barrier with a thump and slowed to snail pace within only a few seconds. It then headed upwards again. He heard Mandy say, "It will do these five times per trip." Stevie's heart was pounding as they headed to the queue to buy their ticket.

Fifteen minutes later it was all over, Stevie's legs were weak under him as they headed out. Mandy clung to him for dear life but he was too busy trying to fight his vomiting to notice. Now he knew why she said that he shouldn't eat the hotdog earlier. He was as white as a ghost. But several minutes later, with bravado, he muttered something like, "That was cool, we should do it again sometime". At the same time, he was thinking I hope I never see that thing again in my life. Mandy giggled and made the comment, "Every time I go on it, I swear it will be my last, but sucker me, I've now done it four times".

They headed into a cafeteria for a soft drink. Stevie's nausea was diminishing and his manhood kept intact. Now euphoric after having survived 'The Thumper'. They giggled and chatted gaily. Until Mandy asked, "How are you going reading that boring physics book that you got from the library?" She then added, "I could never read anything like that with interest."

Stevie went quiet and Mandy could tell that there was something wrong, "Well, what's the matter?"

"Joe found me reading the book and took it from me. He said "'Don't pretend you like this stuff'", and as he did, he ripped it up. Now I have to go to the library and pay for the book."

Mandy kept quiet, but took his hand. Stevie went on, "When I grow up, I will never be like them. I will not drink alcohol, or smoke cigarettes, and I will read and grow my brain". He fell silent.

Trying to lighten the mood Mandy said, "I am going to be a psychologist or a doctor. I want to help people". At that moment Stevie believed she would be that. He felt better knowing that one day he will have control of his life.

What a joke, Stevie thought as he came back to the reality of the moment. That was a lovely day, and he often thought of it with fondness. Mandy went on, not to be a doctor but an anthropologist, and me… I… became Joe…

Stevie's frustration removed him from the hospital and back to the forest, brutalized by the experience.

∞

He immediately set off walking to assuage his sadness, heading roughly to the north. Yes, I became like Joe. The thought saddened him and he tried to stop this train of thought by listening to the crunch of his shoes as we walked on the leaves, and twigs. He would listen and get absorbed, but after ten or so steps he found his mind back to that thought about Joe, and of seeing Mandy in the ward. There was something nagging at his mind, what was it? What was it… Mandy said something… yes, she said, *"… when you had your gloomy periods? You have always been prone to depression."* He had never thought of his moods as depression. After all, depression happens to other people. Not to young people, not to me, he thought.

He stopped and looked forward into the forest, a thousand trees, all looking pretty similar. Could easily get lost in this he thought. It was overcast, and he was sure that the forest had many moods. He did not particularly like it when it was dark like this. He disliked it when it rained, was damp, cold and dark – somehow it took on a sinister feel to it. But when the sun shone it was lovely, giving it such vitality, the leaves appeared silver from the sunlight, especially if there was a light breeze to animate the silver. The blue above and the shafts of light made it friendly.

How can it feel so different? The forest was the forest, irrespective of the light quotient? Then he realised that his body and mind are similar to the forest in as much as the moods seem to be influenced by outside influences.

∞

As Mandy sat there, she felt that she was not alone, but looking around she saw she was. Come on, pull yourself together she thought. As she turned back to Stevie, her mind went to a time when she and Stevie were kids, it was the day they went to the amusement park. Funny she had not thought of that day for years. "You ninny", she softly said to Stevie as she remembered how green he looked after The Thumper.

E M E R G E N C Y   R O O M ...
S U N D A Y 6 : 3 1 A M

Before Rose went home, she conferred with the nurse who was to take over the shift, Nurse Hamlin. "I don't know why but I just feel that we must hold this one a bit longer. So, please, Vicky, let's see if we can keep him going for a while."

"Sure lovey," replied Vicky, but knew it was a waste of time, especially with a Glasgow Coma Scale reading of two.

∞

"I can't get up, I can't breathe. Help!" Stevie shouted.

Stevie struggled to sit up. His arms did not have the power to raise himself from the ground. What breath he had came in gasps. Looking up he could just make out the grey blob that was sitting on his chest and leaning into his face, the smell was overpowering. Becoming frantic he struggled harder but was constrained as if gravity pinned him down. It then shrieked, "We are your fear, come to say hello."

"Ohhhh nooooo," Stevie moaned in terror.

When he awoke the thing was gone. Still sweating and shaking he collapsed back to the ground. Did that happen or was I dreaming, he wondered. Stevie knew he was not dreaming – it was too real.

Drained, he tried to recall what it looked like but only had a vague notion of a blob of dust, and the revolting smell.

∞

Weishka started a conversation, "When they declare your body dead, if you don't return, will you have your body parts donated – after all they may help someone have a better life."

When Stevie had seen the interaction with the doctor and the nurse, the doctor mention donorship. At the time Stevie ignored the implication, but now Weishka bought it up again, but he was smart enough to see it for what it was and replied, "They can do with my body what they want as I have no more use for it."

∞

Hiking that afternoon was meaningless for Stevie. He could not get Mandy out of his mind. Those tears… the sadness. Wish I hadn't seen that, better off not knowing. Maybe I should listen to the Bushman and go back. Perhaps it will be better with what I have seen and learnt… Nah, that stuff may work over here, but on Earth I have my doubts. The old man has shown me many things but in the long run, life there is too difficult.

Being negative, it was another foodless day.

But his thoughts drifted…

∞

Late, that afternoon, "Weishka, please tell me about your life as a Bushman of the Kalahari."

Weishka was delighted and said, "I can't tell you without a fire. Let me show you how to build one."

"Without matches?"

"Just watch," smiled Weishka, "and I'll show you."

Stevie was amazed at how easy it was. First, he had to find a flat piece of wood, about the same size as his palm. He was to get a short round stick. To smooth out the bends and knots he rubbed it on a rock. Dry grass completed the collection. Next, he was told to set a small fire with kindling in a pyramid shape. "Make sure there is lots of air in between, and dry grass," said his mentor.

Weishka guided Stevie to gouge out a small hole in the flat piece of wood. This had to be the same diameter as the stick and not very deep. He did this with a sharp stone. Placing the stick in the hole and the dry grass at the base of the stick, Weishka placed his hands against each other as if to clap with the stick in the middle and vigorously rubbed his hands back and forth, turning the stick in the hole.

Two or three minutes later a wisp of smoke rose from the friction of the two pieces of wood. As it got stronger, the dry grass smouldered and ignited. Weishka put the smouldering grass on the set fire and gently blew to ignite the pile. As it did, he encouraged the fire to grow by placing larger pieces of wood on it. With face beaming, Weishka handed Stevie the two pieces of wood and advised, "Always carry some twigs and dry grass to use when needed."

Half an hour later, sitting in front of the fire, Weishka said, "There are several names for the Bushmen. Some called themselves the San. Others the Khoisan or Koi, depending on which area or clan that one belonged to. So, I suppose the term the Bushman is more of a collective one. It is a term that I like as we are people of the bush. We roamed the Kalahari, an area vaster than the United Kingdom. We Bushmen treat everything with sacredness. Even this fire, it would be wasteful to have a large fire that consumes a lot of wood… Stare into the fire with your eyes and mind... when you look into the coal, you see the sun, for the coal and the sun are one. The sunlight helped grow the trees, then they rotted to become coal, so coal is past sunlight, or stored sunlight.

When you sit close to glowing embers, the sun is close to you. It invites you into a different consciousness."

Weishka's voice was soft and gentle, "We are part of the oldest race in the world... we are the last of the ancient Stone Age people that covered much of Africa. Each clan is made up of about thirty people, but we would rather call it a family as we…" …looking into the fire Stevie saw shimmering colours and shapes, twisting, rising and dropping, yellow and red, white… before he knew it, he had slipped into another world.

"Come," said Weishka, "it's time to join the hunt."

∞

They were in a dry land, so still it could have been a painting. The terrain undulated and was covered in red dirt. Trees were sparse and stubby, an acacia thorn. This would not look strange on Mars, thought Stevie.

He saw a young and strong Weishka, but unlike his elder mentor he wore no clothes. It was good to see him without the need of the stick. He was at the peak of his physical powers – beautiful, standing tall and proud. He was with other tribe members. One gave Stevie what he later learnt was a typical Bushman greeting, raising his right arm high above his head and with palm open said, "Tshjamm" (greetings).

"Tshjamm Nxeu," Stevie returned. He was amazed that he knew their Ikung language (the language of Khoisan of the northern Kalahari) and the man's name. He knew all of their names.

They chattered and laughed a lot, much like he had heard Weishka laugh a hundred times. It was more of a cackle than a deep-throated laugh that blended into the wide expanse that surrounded them. When they spoke, it was with a clicking sound. Stevie was able to follow the conversation, they were speaking of the hunt that they were about to go on.

Like Weishka, their skin was more apricot colour as opposed to the dark of most African skin; all were short and had the fine features of a Gazelle, rather than the large shoulders and thick legs common to the continent. Their face was Mongolian-like and the skin of the face was unbelievably wrinkled from the harsh African sun. Obviously, the trait of smiling was common to the tribe. Stevie was aware of their odour, it had the essence of earthiness about it – archaic and provocative but not offensive.

All carried a bow and a quiver full of arrows. Some had a fur waist band, probably from one of the many varieties of buck that roam the area. From the belt hung arrows or drinking straws.

Crouching over eland hoof prints they explained to Stevie that Eland were special and sacred. "They are animals of mystical power that are sometimes embodied by a shaman that has gone to the spirit world. Being sacred we don't hunt them very often. But we have been given a message that today we must hunt one and take on its spirit from its flesh. Tonight, we will celebrate that spirit."

Crouching around the spore a discussion took place. They seemed to not have a chief and all had a say. Stevie noticed they kept looking to Weishka, whom they obviously held in high regard. The discussion was to determine the identity of the eland they would take. The prints indicated the size, age, sex and health or wellbeing, as well as the direction travelled. They explained that this eland was weak and dragged a leg. It would only be a matter of time before the animal succumbed to Africa's harshness.

After the selection they set off at a trot. Stevie was elated as he was able to keep up with the hunt, even though they trotted. All morning they ran with determination, but the herd seemed to remain distant to them. Every so often one member would stop, check the spoor and report the latest information. Weishka seemed to be the strongest as he was always at the front to point the way. Sometime in the mid-afternoon they gained on the herd. An hour later they could see them. With guile they got close to the beautiful beasts. They were large strong animals, much larger than a cow, but much bigger. They held their heads up high as if to show off their massive antlers. Vertical lines on their hide, like tracks on a map, added to their beauty.

Weishka pointed out to Stevie the selected eland. Crouching, they ran towards it. For a time, the eland ran with the herd. Stevie was appalled to see his companions run into the middle of the panicked herd, where charging eland stormed like runaway cars. Dust rose to the air. Weishka was laughing and treated it as a game as he side-stepped an antelope at the last minute. They took this risk to isolate the candidate. Stevie could see that the eland had a slight limp and was slower than the rest of the herd. It was then he remembered the spore reading; that this one was wounded and was picked for this reason. Even though he would not last long in the wild, the bull was still strong and determined and took off to get back into the retreating pack. The Bushman had to run like the wind to catch him. Stevie, like the rest, was exhilarated.

It was not long before several arrows found the target. Even though these were tipped with poison it would take time to affect such a large animal. But after a time, the prize started to weaken and slowed down enough for Nxeu to race in, and with arm raised high, thrust his spear straight into the heart. Still, this noble beast kept its head raised. Fortunately, it was not long before the others came and put the animal out of its pain.

It seemed to Stevie that the hunter and the hunted entered a sacred partnership where the hunted was subservient to the needs of the hunter, where on a spiritual level the Eland was prepared to sacrifice its life for the welfare of the Bushman, where the consciousness of the animal will continue in some other plane or form. In turn, the Bushman acknowledged and respected the sacrifice and treated the hunt with reverence, knowing that its meat, is their life, and that without this bond they would not exist. Stevie could see the sacred in the relationship, and that the hunt is in fact a ritual.

No sooner than the great beast was dead they started the skinning. Being so large it took several hours to skin and to cut up the meat. Then to Stevie's mind an amazing thing happened – bush people, not only from Weishka's clan but from other clans arrived to help carry and re-ceive meat. He asked, "How did they know that the kill had been made?" He was told they sent mind-talk telling the people of the kill. Stevie thought that even here, these Stone Age people use telepathy.

On their way back the group veered, and then after a few hundred metres stopped for much-needed water. Stevie was thirsty but could not see any ponds or creeks. His hunting friends could see his confusion and laughed, not to mock but for the fun of it. Bauxhau pulled out what looked like a stick from his sisal-like hair. But upon looking closer, Stevie could see that it was a reed straw. Kneeling and using his hands, Bauxhau dug a small hole, and as he did moisture seeped into it. Using the straw, they all had a turn to suck up water. When it was Stevie's turn, they showed him to keep the straw in the water but above the sand to avoid sucking in sand. When finished he stood, his thirst satisfied.

Stevie was given a bow and arrow and told to pretend that the closest tree was an eland and that he must hit it. Thinking that it would be easy, he pulled back the string and aimed the arrow. But instead of the arrow heading straight and true, it wobbled and drifted sideways, like a drunken dirigible, only to fall to the dirt halfway to the tree. At first there was silence but when Stevie laughed all the others to join in. Weishka patted his back affectionately and smiled.

On the way back to the settlement, there was much banter and they kept referring to Stevie as Lxeua. One little hunter kept enacting the feeble wobble of the arrow with such mirth he could hardly stand up. Lxeau, Stevie learnt, means sideway arrow.

"Don't worry," supported Weishka, by being given a name you have been accepted in their ranks as an equal. Forever you will be rewarded with the privileges of a clan member. Your name of Lxeua is a happy one. Nxeu means wooden bowl, and Bauxhau is the stone axe. So Lxeua, enjoy your status as an honorary Bushman."

∞

They were almost upon the settlement before Stevie noticed it – six dome-roofed, grass shanties. Some of the huts had meat hanging to dry in the heat and breeze.

Stevie noticed that the floors of the huts had been scooped out to make sleeping more comfortable and smiled to himself when he thought of his burrows. The children and woman were shy but not scared. Wanting to see, most squatted and watched the hunters.

Like the men, all the women and children were nude. Some of the women also had a skin belt around their waste. Many wore a headband and ankle bracelet made of crushed ostrich egg-shell. Stevie could see that ostrich shells were important as there was a row of them in the shade against the huts. He was told that they stored water.

He watched an aged woman pound some sort of grain in a large stone pestle, using a wooden mortar. Her skin was so weathered it was mummy-like. As she worked, she chatted with those around her, her toothless smile told of some long-known joke. The voices, although not loud carried great distances. Stevie learnt that she was Weishka's mother.

Stevie and Weishka watched the joyful preparation of meat and the feast that was to follow. They sat in the sand, the dying sun caressing their skin with a golden sheen. It was peaceful sitting under a prickly acacia tree whilst gazing at the terrain beyond. Here and there a rocky outcrop rose to break the flat expanse, all covered in the same golden sheen with shadowed crevices.

"Why are there hardly any implements or possessions?" Stevie wondered.

Weishka, picking up the thought, told him, "We Bush people travel light and so keep possessions to a minimum."

"And how come I don't see any pregnant women. How does the clan continue?"

"We are in tune with the seasons and weather patterns and as we are soon to enter a period of drought there will be less food. This could threaten the survival of the clan. More children will come as the drought ends."

Stevie was silent whilst another thought formed in his mind, "When you and the others were dodging the panicked eland herd, how did you and the rest have no fear? If it was me, I'd shit myself."

Weishka burst out laughing before answering. "From the time a child is born, he or she is shown fear is like the light of a fire on the ground. It is there but not there. The light from the torch is also not real. After all, can you catch the light in a bucket? No, you can't, nor can you feel it; there is no heat or cold from it. Fear is the same. It is there but not real. From childhood we Bush people are taught that fear protects us and so we respect fear when it comes. But we do not let it rule us and know how to overcome its power. We face it as we face our image in the river. Remember on your first night you followed my stick and saw me as a small child and how scared I was to walk backwards on the rock. That is the start of the training for the young ones?"

"Yes, I remember. Wish I had been taught those things," said Stevie.

Both were quiet until Weishka asked, "What do you see that stands out the most with my people?"

"I guess I see happiness."

"Yes. We are not only happy today because of the hunt, we are always happy. If we have or not have food or water, we remain happy. Believe me; we have more challenges here in our life than you do in yours. But we don't let an overriding apprehension consume our mind, so our mind can focus on survival and happiness… We call our happiness to us, as without it, we would cease to exist".

Stevie pondered for a minute before making a statement and then asked a question, "I find it interesting that in most Western societies we thank God for the food we have, but you people thank the animal. Is there a difference?"

"Yes and no. No, in as much as by thanking The Intelligence you also thank the animal, or even the plant. But by doing so much of the symbiotic relationship with the animal or plant is not bypassed. Our people, and all indigenous peoples have reverence for that symbiotic relationship – one simply can't exist without the other. It is this loss of understanding of the symbiotic that separates modern society from the old. It is also this loss that has virtually destroyed the planet. It stems from the fact that you see animals as a lower form of life… … I want you to try something Stevie. I want you to address all animals, plant life, and microscopic life with reverence, and when you do it will change you. There will be a psychological change in you."

Stevie made a mental note to do so, but after a few minutes of silence, Stevie spoke, "From my time here I see so much respect for nature, not just the trees but everything. How do I get to know or believe there is spirit in nature?"

Weishka was slow to answer, and then said, "Imagine if you personified the parts of Mother Nature, such as the trees, the rocks, flowers, and water, and love them as the old people did. Modern people do not see beyond their immediate need of the sky, sun or moon. They see a tan from the sun, the sky is something to fly across, and the moon is an organ that helps to seduce a pretty woman. But if only they stopped and gave a face to Mother Nature, a personality, all would change for them. The grandmother who spoilt you and gave you gifts is very real to you. Why is not Grandmother Moon real to you? She should be as real as your grandmother. The same with Grandfather Sun, his gift of warmth and growth are just as real as your grandfather's stories."

Weishka continued but changed the subject again to say, "For thousands of years our people foraged and hunted in the greater Kalahari and lived a life of spiritual connection to the land. We travelled with migrating herds where the clan all contributed to the benefit of all. Although we kept to ourselves, we welcomed all travellers into our midst and respected all cultures. We are, and always have been, passive and peace loving, which was different to the aggressive war-like tribes of the time. We are appalled at the thought of killing another human. Animals are only killed for food and pelts, and always as quickly as possible".

"So", Stevie asked, "what is the problem with modern man, and why is life on Earth so full of war, hate, greed… lust… and … and I guess fear?"

"Simple, man has lost his connection to all that is sacred. You are starting to see that sacredness is a fact. You see the vibration of people and animals… see what negativity does to a life, your life for instance. Seeing the sacred is being in awareness, with respect. This keeps one in the right vibration, to be in the sacred. It is this that mankind has lost… they are in the wrong vibration."

"Do you think that modern humanity has the capacity to save the earth from devastation?"

"No… There are many that talk but do nothing themselves. Consumerism and hunger for more is what drives humanity. The need for more is too entrenched."

"You paint a grim picture Weishka".

"Perhaps, but it is quite simple, man collectively, and individually does not have the 'will' to change himself to change the planet… it is just a matter of time…' Having said his bit, Weishka got up and went to play with some of the children, leaving Stevie to enjoy the moment.

Watching the preparations, it seemed to him that the clan never ate all their food in one sitting and always kept some for another day. Spare meat was quickly cut into strips and hung to dry. Nothing was wasted or discarded, except for the dung in the stomach. The entrails were cleaned and preserved, the half-digested vegetable matter and moisture was squeezed out and saved in an open ostrich shell for drinking.

Bauxhau came over, "Tshjamm Lxeua".

"Tshjamm Bauxhau", Stevie returned, as he patted the sand next to him for Bauxhau to sit with him.

For a moment they sat in comfortable silence, until Bauxhau said, "Tonight we are going to dance. We cannot take such a great animal without gratitude and praise for its sacrifice. Come and join us in the preparation."

∞

At first the dance was of a slow rhythm as they thanked the soul of the eland. But as night advanced, the dance quickened as it was charged with energy for the seeking of mystical things. Many whirled, whilst others pounded the ground with heavy feet. After a time, several dancers collapsed, not with fatigue but in trance. A shaman with glazed eyes went to a sick child and drew out the demon that ailed her. So removed from physical life, many danced in the flames and coals of the fire without harm. Weishka told Stevie that there is wisdom in flame and that flame is a benevolent entity.

There is no doubt that all felt The Intelligence and communed directly with it. Every so often he would hear the word "n/um". Each time it was shouted it was always with reverence. Not knowing what it meant he would later ask Weishka.

Stevie whirled and danced with them. Soon he was without existence, he was just millions of molecules that mixed with the molecules of everything around him. All he was, was consciousness. He was the consciousness of the trees, and the bush. He was the consciousness of the animals. There was though, another aspect of that consciousness that, at first subtle, grew stronger as he became more familiar – and was love. It pervaded everything. Never had Stevie experienced anything as joyous as this.

Beyond the light of the fire, hyenas growled as if to join the group in their sacred search. Owls hooted, and jackals howled to the moon. Further away, the deep-chested roar of a lion could be heard. Towards the end of the ceremony, Nxeu picked up some red coals in his bare hands and scattered them far and wide for all in the world to share. As they landed in the dark, they appeared to be like stars in the constellation.

"Come Lxeua… Sideway Spear," laughed Weishka, "back to your own journey."

∞

In his forest as Stevie had come to think of it, he thought of what he had learnt from these Stone Age child-men. So many lessons of the humble connection to nature and the land that supports them. Since he had started his etheric journey, one of the main things that Weishka tried to impart was to trust that all will be given. Certainly, the Bushmen trusted the land to supply, and it seemed to him that it did. He also learnt about fear and that it is only as real as he wanted it to be. And then he considered what Weishka said about, "calling their happiness", that without it, they would not exist as a clan. Certainly, it would have made their harsh life bearable. The seeing and feeling of all, as if he was 'The Intelligence' – he witnessed the very creation he lived in.

Stevie was concerned for the planet and all that lived on it

EMERGENCY ROOM ...
SUNDAY 7:48 AM

As the doctor on duty checked Stevie's chart, she moaned to herself, "Typical of the night shift to leave us to clean this one up. Well, I'll only organize the Neuro-response test when I get a chance."

Seeing a young woman sitting in the visitors' chair, she asked, "You a relative?"

Mandy saw the name Doctor Moses on her name. "Sort of. How is he doing?"

The doctor did not have the heart to say that they would soon take him off life support but mumbled, "Not too good I'm afraid," and hurried off to another bed.

∞

The next morning Stevie awoke to cloud cover but there was no immediate threat of rain. His hunger pains reminded him to keep positive, trust and love. He remembered the conversation with Weishka about knowing the contents of his mind and how easy it is to change when aware. Practicing this, he kept saying to his mind, "I am happy, I trust, I love," and when he did this, he sent love to himself. Before long, indeed, he felt better.

It was not long when he saw a ground bird running before him. Thinking it was a pheasant he chased it and ran as fast as he could but the bird had evaded faster and more agile predators than Stevie and so easily got away, but not before leading Stevie to a pond. Laughing and puffing at the futility of the chase he sat by the water. Looking into it he saw large trout-like fish, sunning itself on the surface. The water did not seem to be deep. Picking up a stone he took careful aim – whack! A direct hit along the ridge line on the head. As he grabbed the stunned fish he offered, "Sorry," in gratitude.

The sun finally broke through the cloud and did not take long to scorch. Next to the pond there was black shale that had heated like a hot plate. Stevie put the fish on this and using a stick, pushed it flat. Every so often he turned it over and moved it to another hot section of rock.

Thirty minutes later he licked the last of the fish off his fingers. He thought of the way he was led to the fish. Only after he was in a happier state of mind, did he see the bird. There was never a hope of catching it but it led him to the pond. When about to throw the stone, he had no doubt that he would hit the fish, which was now satisfyingly in his stomach. He remembered what Weishka said about how the receiving of abundance was not always in the form asked for – he was after a ground-bird, and ended up with a fish.

Could be… just could be that the Weishka is right about manifesting!

∞

"Weishka…I have a question that I have wanted to ask you for some time."

With his ever-present smile, Weishka raised an eyebrow to indicate to Stevie to go ahead.

"When we had that first conversation you said that my life did not work because I lived it badly or something like that. Can you elaborate?"

"Yes, that's true, and the technical reason is that your personality or human vibration did not match your soul vibration."

"Eh?" thought Stevie.

"I'll explain. Your soul is geared for one main focus, and that is to move closer to The Intelligence. It can only do that when you live with joy, love and spiritual balance. These are positive vibrations within a specific range. As you have learnt, the opposite is fear and you predominately lived in the range of fear and anger. We have spoken about people having free will, which means that they determine their own vibrational frequency, as you just said. There can be, and in your case, there was, an incongruence between your soul identity and your physical identity. For a life to work, you need to be in universal flow, which means matched frequency."

Stevie thought about this for a time. Then he chuckled as he remembered what Weishka said about a mind full of questions; "I get that and it makes sense but now I have another question for you. What is astral travelling?"

"Some call it 'out-of-the-body experience'. The astral body may be defined as the double or ethereal body. This is the etheric counterpart of the physical body. It has also been known as the mental body, the spiritual body, the subtle body, the shining body and various other names. The name is not important; however, its capabilities are. It can and does remove itself from the physical body. In this realm you will have noticed that this body is non-material, meaning that it is not solid like your body – most of matter seems to be real in your life. If you go back to your incarnation, you can learn to astral trav…"

Stevie was so excited with this thought that he interrupted Weishka mid-word, "You serious? This could be great." But then he remembered that he may not go back. "Sorry, I interrupted you."

Weishka carried on, "All your religious texts talk about a physical and spiritual body, such as the reference by Paul in his first Epistle to the Corinthians. Psychic research has been ongoing and has established the truth that within every material being there is a non-material double. I am also sure that you have heard stories of people who have seen a relative who is known to be some distance away, perhaps fighting a war. This person appears to them for a short period of time only to disappear as soon as they are seen. The confused host would later hear of the death of that relative on that distant battle ground at that same time. This is body projection by the dead person in a last-minute attempt to reach or say goodbye to his loved ones.

All people astral project or travel at various times throughout their lives…

Only most do not remember. The projection can happen in many ways but when back in the body no memory of it is held. There are some, the likes of yogis and mediums, who have trained themselves to consciously remember their travels.

There are also times when people have out-of-body experiences as a result of a bang on the head or an accident. These are commonly called near-death experiences and are always involuntary. It can sometimes be induced by hypnotic suggestion or deep meditation.

You did this after you collapsed unconscious, before coming to this plane. Remember, it was when you first saw your body separate from yourself."

"If I was to return to my body… remember this is only hypothetical as I am not going to… would I remember my out-of-body times," asked Stevie.

"Yes, if you have the desire, and by doing so you could benefit from the experience as it could help with your growth and understanding. As a traveller, you would be able to go to many realms. This will contribute to your store of knowledge but also helps to confirm the oneness of all."

"What is the cord that is attached to my body? I saw it on my last visit to my hospital bed?"

"The cord is a good name. It is attached to your medulla oblongata at the back of your head. This keeps you attached to your physical body so that you can re-enter it when required."

"What happens if it gets cut or separated?" Stevie asked.

"Your material body dies and decomposes. The only difference between astral projection, and what you call death, is the cord… Before the start of your journey I warned you that if you don't get back to your body in time then you will be locked out – your cord will detach or disintegrate."

Stevie shuddered.

EMERGENCY ROOM …
SUNDAY 10:12 AM

Mrs Jones rang the hospital to find out how Stevie was getting on. The nurse was to the point, "It's unlikely he will come out of the coma. If you want to see him, you'd better hurry."

So here she was standing next to his bed. She knew the implication of the virtual flat line and wondered if she had found him earlier, would it have made a difference. A few minutes later a nice-looking girl came in. "Hi, I'm Elaine Jones."

"I'm Mandy, nice to meet you."

"Oh, *you're* Mandy… I wondered what happened to you… as he spoke highly of you, and I might add often, very often."

A nurse with 'Victoria' on her name tag came in to bring fresh water in a glass jug. Bit pointless, she thought, this guy's not drinking again.

"Nurse," asked Mrs Jones, "is there anything else that can be done for Stevie?"

"Don't ask me, I'm just a nurse. You will have to ask the doctor on duty." And with that she left.

Mrs Jones already knew the answer. Mandy had become quiet and did not seem to want to talk to a stranger. For her part Mrs Jones was satisfied to have quiet as she was saying goodbye to Stevie in her own way.

∞

Stevie had been walking all morning. He carried the awareness of Weishka's suggestion of holding all that he came in contact with reverence. He had noticed that there was a subtle change to the way he perceived things. At first, he could not put his figure on it but there was definitely something to it. After a time, he realised that by showing reverence he was making a connection across consciousness. Perhaps, by feeling the reverence he was matching his vibration to that which he focused on. Weishka has been saying all along that every living thing has consciousness, that all is connected, and that all you have to do is look for it and the connection will become obvious. He was seeing and feeling what he had always been connected to but did not recognise the connection. He also remembered what Weishka said about modern mankind, that they created the current chaos of life because they have lost their connection.

He sat on a rock to marvel about this, and as to how blind he and the rest of mankind had been. His thought was interrupted with what he realised was a telepathic message; *'I'm dying, slowly dying – yet nobody listens, nobody cares.*

The tragedy is not only about me. It's about all the animals that live on me, the fish in the sea, the birds, bunnies and penguins, the poor lizards and lovely beetles. All will perish with me – all species will be gone forever.

And what about me? I have a soul and I have feelings. I don't want to die. Yet my veins are full of poisons and my air, which was once so clean and pristine, is now murky and heavy. Not to mention the toxins that have killed the goodness of my soil. The aura that surrounds me is lifeless, all color gone.

The trees and plants are dwarfing and suffocating, dying of the same cancer as I am.

We had a deal, you and I – I would let you live here… on me, but only if you respected me. Part of our deal was that you would bathe in the enchantment of what I had to offer, glory in my beauty and abundance as God's art.

But you have destroyed me. Like a young and innocent girl, you have whored me, brutalised me and left me to lie in my own vomit, too weak and sick to help myself. You changed the environment so what was once controlled is now out of control. Yes, it is you, man, who has caused the wind to destroy, rain to flood, and sun to dry, desecrate and burn.

I cry tears of anguish for the lost future – do you not realize what you have done? How can you be so shallow in your outlook? Your law of Thou shall not kill is ignored when it comes to me, your mother, as every day the stake is driven deeper and the gases become more intoxicating. My death is slow and full of pain. I am not meant to die. Not yet, anyway. I trusted man. I did not know that you were without a soul, callous and uncompromising.

In generations to come, when I am a lifeless, barren ball of darkness, somberly floating through the universe, the annals of history will show that man was the selfish race… But you Stevie… you can make a difference, you can tell the world what you have seen… yes… you are only one, but you if you have the will you can make a difference."

∞

Stevie had difficulty sleeping that night and was glad to get out of his burrow to get going. He was all too aware of the grim prediction that Weishka made, when he said he felt mankind to entrenched in want, greed, and consumerism to reverse the process. Stevie also remembered the conversations of collective energy, and that if somehow mankind could all feel as he is feeling now, and as he did when at the Bushmen's fire – then it could turn around. But, as Weishka said the collective consciousness of mankind is one of negativity.

He walked hard, as if to purge himself, and all mankind of their foolish ways. Never again will he take things for granted. But after about four hours of walking he came to a plateau that overlooked a valley far below. Tall and bushy trees gave good shade. The cliffs were light sandstone. These contrasted with the green of the distant valley. Picking a flat rock to sit on, he looked at the view and thought how lovely this is, just like Earth. As he looked over the expanse, the words, *"I'm dying, slowly dying – yet nobody listens, nobody cares…* filled his mind.

Taking his water bottle out of his bag he took a drink. The ever-busy mind wondered if there would be karma to mankind for destroying the planet, their home. He realised that knowing this put additional pressure on him. He *should* go back to his body to tell mankind what they are doing to Mother Earth… I don't want this responsibility. He wanted to remove this from his mind and so he asked, "Weishka, what is karma really about? Are we ruled in this life from issues that we carried over from a past life? I'm not sure if I believe in it."

"Yes, but many let the knowledge of this rule their lives… For instance, let's assume that a person believes that he has a karma issue coming through from a past life. The person has a choice, to either let the issue rule their current life or to overcome it. Most let the issue rule them, after all, being with the karma or fate, there is nothing they can do about it… thereby creating an uncomfortable life. But it does not have to be like this, as once you are aware of an issue, by sending love to it, it can be melted."

"I don't understand. Can you explain further?"

"Alright. let's say that a man commits a crime, perhaps armed robbery. For this he is sent to jail for twenty years. In year nineteen he escapes. In the eyes of the law, and society, he has not served his term. People equate the laws of karma much as the laws of humanity, in that all past deeds must be fully accounted for. This is not the case with karma. A deed, any deed from a past life or period in this life, irrespective of how terrible it may have been can be dissolved, especially by sending it love… by being compassionate, generosity…"

"Eh, send it love?"

"Yes, you send it love. Let me give you another example. Assume that in the past you raped a girl and at the time, and afterwards, you held no concern for the girl's emotional or physical pain. You had no remorse. Then in this life, you kept meeting girls who were unfaithful to you, bullied you, and treated you with disrespect. If you were able to see the link between the past-life events and see the pattern of events of all the callous woman that you attracted, then that would be a start. The second step is to acknowledge your past behaviour, ask for forgiveness from the girl and then forgive yourself. At the same time, you send love, the most powerful force there is. By sending love to the girl that you raped, and the other girls, whilst at the same time sending love to yourself, will transmute the bad karma. That's all, quite simple really."

"Easy, you have got to be joking."

Weishka laughed, "Stevie, I can tell you, it does get easy with practice... It is the way of the Universe, the law or the Intelligence. There is another way to clear karma and that is through service."

"What sort of service?"

"Help people, charitable deeds whilst not expecting a reward. By doing this with a warm heart is the cure of karma. Or, as you just had the thought, the one you wanted to avoid, of going back to earth and telling all about what you have seen of the decline of Mother Earth."

"You really believe that you can change the effects of fate as deemed from a past-life issue?"

"Yes, you can...but there is no such thing as fate. Fate is a cop-out used by humans to avoid responsibility. These people think that a nasty issue must be divinely orchestrated. I can tell you that you exert control over your own life through acknowledging the process and the sending of love. Fate is only fate if you believe it to be so."

"Can you tell me if I have any bad karma?"

"Hmmm..." Weishka mused, "Everybody has karma of one sort or another. Remember, it could be good karma, as not all karma is negative. When you were at your body, you saw that nurse called Rose tending to you far more than the job entails. Every time she puffs up your pillow or mopes your brow with concern, she is creating good karma. Compassion is good karma, as is all 'service'. You must look at all karma as a lesson."

EMERGENCY ROOM...
SUNDAY 3:19 PM

For the second time Dr Moses headed towards the bed of Steven Jardine, but like the first, there was a call over the intercom, "Doctor Moses, please come to emergency, Doctor Moses... You are wanted in the nurse's area."

Well he's already dead, she thought to herself, and so he's not going anywhere. Besides, we need him on support to keep the organs alive for the donor programme.

∞

The sky held a few wisps of cloud, floating like puffs of smoke, but after a time thickened and became solid and menacing. The wind picked up and howled. This is going to be some storm, thought Stevie. Wanting to practice his new skill of manifesting, he sent love for a place of shelter to emerge. As the storm built up, he kept walking and determinedly remained in trust that a place would be presented.

After a time, he felt compelled to head towards a high clump of trees over to his right. As he got there the pent-up storm released itself with fury, trees bent and branches swung wildly as if mechanical. Even though it was day, the light was gloomy, except when dazzling, and sharp cracks of lightening seared the sky.

Stevie found shelter in the roots of a massive tree. It had a girth at its base the size of a large car, and had long ago been hollowed out by ants as a nest. It seemed to welcome him as the storm raged. The storm bought cold, but the tree had absorbed the earlier warmth of the sun, and with the protection of the wind, was womb-like and comforting. He was lulled into a sense of security. He considered this secure state, to the one that he had lived when in his body.

"Weishka, how do I release my anger?"

Weishka thought for a second then said, "I want you to bring to your mind an event that you felt you had no power over."

Immediately an event came to his mind, which he related to Weishka.

"Where we grew up there was a forest in which we used to play Cowboys and Indians. We were rough and at times got hurt. I remember one day my friend John came in with an arrow sticking out of his head… well, it was embedded in his cheek and kind of wobbled up and down as he moved. Anyway, there was a time when in a skirmish, I hit David Bar. I remember his name because we used to call him baa-baa from the nursery rhyme. Being the same age as myself it seemed fair to rough him up a bit – boy he was lucky I didn't scalp him. The next day he came with his dad, and as luck would have it, it was at a time when I was completely on my own. My twelve year's of life were no match against a man, and so it was not much of a contest. "Fuck with my boy," he growled, whilst giving me the first slap on the face. This knocked me to the ground. Every time I got up, I was slapped down again, and as he did, he snarled, "You're a worthless piece of shit."

Stevie told Weishka how he was stunned at this brutish behaviour and language from an adult. "Old man Bar did not use a closed fist, as that would have left a mark, but it was gruelling and went on for about twenty minutes. I put up a brave fight, as every time I got up, I would assume the protective boxing stance and try to issue a couple of left jabs in an effort to defend myself. These would have been like being brushed with ostrich feathers, and so cuff, again I would go down. But even so, I did not show any fear or respect to him, nor did I apologize for hurting his son. At any time, I could have just run away, and I'm sure he would not have run after me… I didn't, I hung in there, and this made him madder, which meant the wallops got harder. My anger overwhelmed me and I did my best to beat him up. But what could a twelve-year-old do against a grown man?

Meanwhile, his wimp of a son, David, just stood by watching"

Weishka did not comment on the story but said, "I want you to re-enact the incident, and as you do, I want you to pay attention to any hurt, inadequacy or helplessness you felt. I want you to focus on the inadequacy and anger."

Stevie did, and felt the injustice of it, just as he did at the time. He felt belittled. But Weishka's thoughts consoled him, "Don't give in to the fear. Claim your personal power. Go through each feeling, but this time don't feel inadequate – feel powerful, claim your power and let it swamp the feeling… reducing its hold on you… Now, forgive that man who beat you."

Stevie focused on this and after a time felt better.

"Now forgive yourself for any anger that you directed against him. Let go of your feeling of inadequacy against the power of a grown man. Send love to him… and to yourself… and whilst in a forgiving mind set, I want you to bring the same attention to the incident where Joe took the cat from you."

This was harder for Stevie. Bringing up that emotion was almost too much to bear. He wanted to escape or get it over with. Acid tears burnt his eyes and raced down his cheeks. He felt frustrated and had to bargain with himself to continue the process. His mind kept saying, why are you doing this to yourself?

He felt guilty because he was not able to protect his kitty. Jet relied on him to keep him safe… and he had failed. As he went through the range of emotions, he was able to reduce their hold on him. Weishka gently encouraged, "It's okay Stevie, just let it go. The only power that it has over you is the power that you give it. Remember, you were only twelve years old. Let it go… let it go… Now forgive Joe and Doris… forgive yourself for thinking that you failed the cat. Sometimes there are things that we have no control over and you had no control over Joe. It may seem at odds, but be grateful for the lesson as it will have shown you how your emotions and reactions took your power away."

Stevie nodded but said nothing.

Weishka stood, leaning on his crooked stick but looked Stevie the eye. "You know you have to clear that other issue, don't you?"

For a second or two Stevie looked down at the ground, unable to say anything. Abruptly he got up and said, "Storms finished," and left the safety of the tree.

∞

Upon waking up one morning he watched the sun butter the vegetation with a light yellow. As the rays grew, the plants and flowers seemed to raise their tiny heads to greet and thank the sun.

As Stevie watched, his mind wandered and he realized that he had been on the journey for about nine days, etheric days that is. The thought panicked him. He needed to see if his physical body was still alive.

It was odd watching the coming and going of the medical staff as they checked the monitor and took his pulse. Always they checked his blankets and tucked him in and gave him a quick pat of encouragement as if there was healing in such activities. Perhaps there was. Maybe it is the small things like these that give value to life. Kindness and support from strangers.

And there, still sat Mandy. She held Stevie's hand and only released it to blow a tear-caused runny nose. He wondered what she was thinking. He looked beyond the walls to other patients. Most were fighting for their lives, whilst I scorn mine. In their precarious state, many realised the value of their fragile life, and how precious it is.

He knew that most of them had lived lives that lacked expression. Many were also consumed by fear and self-esteem issues. He could feel the despair that they had for their uncertain future. They wondered – am I going to die? Will there be pain? All were scared. For a minute Stevie wished that he could go to them and show they have nothing to fear.

With this thought came the realization of how much he had learnt on his Journey of Learning.

His focus went back to the Stevie in the bed, he knew what the almost flat line of the monitor meant. He also knew that his body was being depleted of life force. Its energy field still small and insipid with little time before there was no return.

"Weishka, what happens when my body dies… I mean, what happens to me, this me that it is talking to you, not the physical me in the bed?"

The old African had a small smile knowing this question would soon arrive in Stevie's searching mind. "I will explain this to you with a simplistic explanation, which should be adequate for now…

As I said before, your physical body dies when the cord that connects you has been severed. It is not when your heart stops, or your blood pressure drops to nothing. Nor is it when your brain dies... So when the cord is dis-attached, your personality, or the little bit of 'The Intelligence' that resides in you leaves the body in the form of Intelligent Consciousness to remerge with The Greater Intelligence. From there, that Intelligent Consciousness heads up what you have been referring to as 'the tunnel'. Once on that other side, there is a period of adjusting, of resting, and of introspection. This time period is dependent on the life that has just been had. It also depends on the spiritual development that was to be had or gleaned in that life, or before that life. On that other side, time is not the same notion as it is perceived to be here in the physical form. So don't be too worried about that timeframe.

When the Intelligent Consciousness is ready, over a period of time it is supported by advanced spirits in the form of an enquiry of that life... a kind of debrief. This enquiry is gentle but truthful, and the Intelligent Consciousness is a willing participant. And so it goes ahead in a positive and loving manner, where insight and understanding is gained for greater spiritual growth".

Stevie's focus was total, a million questions formed but he held them at bay.

Weishka took a second to organise his thoughts and then continued, "Once a good understanding is derived by the Intelligent Consciousness of that previous life, the lessons learnt, or not learnt, its future is looked at and decided upon by all. What this means is that when the Intelligent Consciousness is ready, it may offer service on that side to human beings on this side or in other realms. But there is likely to be a time when the Intelligent Consciousness assumes another life on earth to further its development".

After clearing his throat, as if to remove a wad of Kalahari dust, his final words were, "I do not want to say much more on this as it is enough for you to consider. But now you can see why I have said several times that if you do not learn the lessons in this life, then you will return until you do".

∞

The next day whilst Stevie hiked, a concept came that intrigued him. Here I am in this etheric form, then who is the Stevie in the hospital? Who am I? he wondered, who is the real me?

Who am I?

I guess I am me. No, that does not sound right.

Who *am* I?

Actually, I don't know who I am.

Who am I?

I'm not my job as a designer. Surely, I am more than that. And if I stopped designing my life would still continue.

Who am I?

Perhaps the personality moulded by my family influence. I don't have to allow myself to remain influenced by that.

And although it rules me, I know that I am not my anger. I'm more than that. In fact, I'm even more lost when in anger.

Then who am I?

I am not my resentment.

Who am I?

Am I child of Universal Intelligence. But what does that mean? Sounds too corny.

Who am I?

He stopped walking to tie up a shoelace. When straightening he took off his hat and wiped the sweat off his brow. As he did, he looked at the bush, the sky and the hills beyond. He felt attuned with them, it was a sunny day, and so it was comforting. He liked that feeling and understood that it had always been there, that is why he has always loved the bush. Replacing his hat, he continued walking.

Who am I?

If I have trillions of cells that die each day, only to be replaced with new ones, then who am? And If I look in the mirror every month, I will see a changing face. Who am I under

the aging skin? Certainly, not my body.

And, if my preferences and thought processes change over time, as they have, then who am I?

I cannot relate to the person who I was when I eight years old? That being the case, who was I then… and who am I now. Who will I be in ten years time – seemingly different people.

There seems to be nothing consistent about myself.

This morning I was grumpy, an hour later happy, then agitated. So if I am not my emotions, then who am I? And if my emotions jump around as they do, how is one ever to understand who one is.

Weishka said that if I was to look at myself under a microscope, magnified a thousand to one, I would see that everything is moving, and would look like those little bubbles in a saucepan when heating up, all bobbling every which way… I saw something similar when in the trance at the Bushmen's fire. So, if my body is not solid matter, then who or what am I.

So… if I have conversations and talk about me or I, who is that?

An now that I am dead, or close to being dead, who would Mandy think I am – I would have to be a construct of her mind, which would have to be subjective. It is also likely

to be different from the one I project of myself.

Then who am I – really?

I must be all my collective experiences and emotions. I suppose that if I let events and my reaction to them rule me, then that could make up who I am…But I must be deeper than that… and if I am deeper, I should be able to reduce the effect of emotions on myself.

If I can't remember most of the days that I have lived, and if memory gives form to my personality, then that can't be accurate. Alternatively, if my memory bank was somehow wiped out, I would lose everything that forms my identity. Who would I be then? No memory means no personality, therefore no me.

But many of my memories are not good memories, so do I want to be that?

There has to be more. Besides, the memory dies when the body dies – nothing left

So, who am I?

For a long time, he had no answer… am I the molecules I saw when in the trance?

Who am I?

I can't be my ego. Weishka says that the ego does not survive death and that it is mortal. Yet a part of me does continue when I die. I could be governed by my ego if I allowed. If that is the case then how do I recognize the part of me that is not ego?

Yes! Yes, that must be it – the part of me that is not the ego.

Then what is that non-ego part?

Striving further he considered the frustration and confusion that seemed to be with him all his life and which probably lead him to commit suicide. If I had found the non-ego aspect of me, then it is unlikely that I would have allowed my life to slide as it did.

Why did I not see that? Did I not want to see it? Who am I that blocks these things?

I don't have to be that pain or confusion. He felt good about this.

Who am I?

Who *am* I?

I don't know who I am. I know who I'm not, but this does not show me who I am. Could it be that I am an aspect of something so great that I have no comprehension of its grander? No frame of reference for me to understand it. That would explain why I can clearly see what I am not, but not what I am. But now I do have an essence of it – most don't.

Yes, with this method of reasoning I can easily see what I am not.

I must be something, otherwise why am I here?

Who am I?

He sat down and closed his eyes so as to be more with the process. Pushing deeper into himself, beyond thought, beyond beliefs, past conditioning, through needs – he saw an aspect of who he is.

I am awareness – the non-ego me.

At this stage Stevie's level of consciousness tapped directly into his higher self. He saw that the end result of this form of enquiry identified his separation of himself or rather his ego from, what Weishka called "The Intelligence", as once ego is removed then it can only be The Intelligence. He realized that it was just a glimpse but it was a start.

But what does the awareness show me?

It shows that all the stuff in my head is stuff of no consequence. This thought gave him a sense of freedom.

So... I'm closer to who I am when in awareness?

Who am I?

I am freedom. But I can only be free when my ego does not command... or demand. This felt good.

Perhaps I am happiness. Yes, I could be... Could I really?

If I am these things, then what is my body for?

It is just a vehicle that allows me to be here so I can experience. He had a saying that he was fond of – that he was born in the city so he could love the bush. Maybe, just maybe, he has a body so he can experience his higher purpose – wow!

The body on its own is of no consequence, only awareness is. But the body is also a receptacle of pain and sickness, which lead the mind to acceptance and understand, whilst remaining connected, or confusion and anguish, and away from awareness.

What about love? At that moment he was swirling in it. It was all around him, was a part of him, like a mist of joy and compassion. He was amazed at how easy it was to be love... now he second experience of it. Behind his closed eyes there was light. He floated with love. He knew that whilst in this state of awareness nothing could touch him. Is this who I am? Is this who I should be? He was not sure but knew it was closer to his core.

But I am in a physical body.

The silence beyond 'stuff' was peaceful and comforting. He felt a hint of belonging there. More than a hint but he could not explain it. This state gave him a hint of what oneness really means.

Who am I? …

Having run out of ideas he continued his walk and felt at peace. But it was not long before he received a thought from Weishka, "I followed your process and was pleased for you. Especially with the understanding that freedom is your right. What you have just seen, is just the edge of alertness. The more you look, the more you will see. It is like a wedge that thickens the further into it you go. The wedge is similar to the soul and the soul is your link to the Intelligence. You became wisdom observing itself, and that is why it felt so good. Spirituality is actively living with this awareness. Each time you ask, 'Who am I?' you further your knowledge. You become open to more questions and answers, and as you learn more, more questions arise.

I have just a few more points to make before I let you continue your hike. The first is that when in awareness as you were just now, there is possibility. In non-awareness there is limitation. In awareness there is love and joy…"

"I now see that," said Stevie excitedly.

"Good. But the love that you felt… it was…" Weishka searched for the perfect words but gave up, "…there are no words in any language that adequately explain the power of universal love. But you sampled it when you saw the light. Enjoy your walking."

Stevie kept pondering these concepts and had another realisation. He just experienced love. He has also experienced extreme fear. On the Earth plane, one must have a body. And if there is a body an ego comes with it. He knows that the ego does perform important functions, such as encouraging us to be the best that we can be, it drives us, which is evolution and self-preservation. But a 'run-away, out of control' ego is a real detriment. So, the trick is to be able to control the ego, and the only way that can happen is with awareness. To do this one would need to develop the ability to be able to live as a normal human with the ego, but to be able to switch to awareness at regular intervals, to be with spirit or love. So, function in ego when doing work or chores but switch to love as often as possible.

∞

It was not long before it became too dark to continue so he settled down on a hillock that overlooked a valley of trees. The ever-present mountains outlined the rim of his view.

Weary from his day, it did not take long to fall asleep but later, damp from the heavy dew, he woke up cold. The full moon gave luminance to the sky. So bright, few stars were visible. The mountains and trees, a dark form against the lighter sky.

He woke again and saw that the moon had shifted its position far to the west. Still too early to get up he slept some more.

At dawn he shivered with cold. Birds chirped as they set about their day. To his right a slither of light grew and clawed its way to prominence. Attached, as if by an invisible rope, was the sun that gave colour and form to the valley below and a distant mountain. As the rope pulled the sun higher, more colour was added until individual trees and rocks could be made out.

He watched all of this with wonder. The birds, now an orchestra, increased their tempo. When the sun finally nosed over the horizon, slithers of light reached across the land, inserting shadows into crevices on the rocks. Suddenly, the sun was fully developed, big, round and bright, warmth fed into him. It reminded him to continue on his way as it is likely to be hot later.

∞

He had been walking for about an hour when he became aware that something was following him – it had been for some time. He heard the occasional crunching of leaves and twigs, the rustling of branches. It seemed to come from the area where the bush was the thickest.

He stopped and listened. Other than the occasional bird, there was silence. But he knew that obnoxious odour.

He carried on and heard the same sound, then pausing in mid-step – silence but still the odour...

Walking again, this time it was the unmistakeable sound of someone or something walking through the bush on a parallel course. Whatever it was, it did not seem to worry about being detected. He started running. So did it. In fact, the combination of the whooshing bush and crunching bark got louder. Risking a look away from the path he was hurtling along, he saw the grass flatten as it kept his pace.

Terrified, he ran as fast as he could. The fear drove his legs faster. They were like pistons as his knees rose and descended. He kept stealing anxious glances and saw the bending and flattening of grass and shrubs as the unseen thing tormented.

Consumed with fear, Stevie had no connection with the ground or of the physicality of the bush. Got to get away… … got to get away. But deep in his mind a memory determinedly fought to reach the surface, like a root pushing through thick soil to light and air. The memory finally broke through his conscious mind to deliver its message.

The first time it was delivered it was soft and made no impression. But whatever the idea was that struggled to be heard, it was determined and so pushed further, until its message was delivered – *face your fear!*

Instantly he stopped, and he heard it again – *face your fear!* For a time, he heard nothing other than his oxygen-depleted breathing. Focusing, he consciously quelled his fear. This was easier to do than he thought, and a calm acceptance came over him.

Once his breath was normal, he looked around for the thing that tormented. There was no sign of it. He sensed that as long as he remained in trust that he was safe. He quickly scanned his energy field and saw that it was almost non-existent. It was ragged and had large holes in it. Cautiously he continued on his way. The bush was peaceful and still.

Even though his heart still pounded, Stevie was elated as by controlling his fear he had dealt with the thing. It was through his own efforts of awareness, and not with the help of Weishka. He had listened and heard his intuition. He wished he had that knowledge when it woke him up that time when it sat on him. He knew a life long fear now had no control over him. He also realised that this was the first time in his life that he has actually stopped to face any fear that he may have had. He had always run, lashed out, got drunk to mask it – anything but face it.

It was then that Weishka's thought came through, "Yes, my boy, I am proud of you. And now look at your vibration."

He did and saw that already it was larger with more colour. The holes filling in.

Aware of being called 'my boy', it felt good but said, "What was that? Surely, I did not imagine it? ...I was terrified, and..."

"Dark forces," replied Weishka. "It was a dark force playing its game."

"What are they?"

Weishka continued, "There are forces that are not benign and seek to control. They do this by sowing fear. Dark is scared of light. When you started this journey, your light was a mere flicker and the dark was not concerned. But as you learnt and developed your light cast further, and so dark wanted to extinguish your light and knows that fear is the best way to do this."

"Like the fear that lived in me?"

"Yes, they come from the same source."

Stevie pondered before asking, "Are these dark forces the devil?"

"Something like that, but there is no devil. The devil is a concept invented by one of your religions to control their members. Some things can't be explained to you, not because we hide it but because they are so distant from your understanding that to explain would leave you more confused than now. But you will understand that dark wants humanity to move farther away from light. They do this by keeping people in fear-induced chaos. The mechanism is fear. As I have said before, and no doubt will say again – fear is a separation from trust. If you look at your life and most of humanity, all live in fear. Just look at the state of your world and you will see what I mean. For hundreds of years there have been wars, famine, sickness, corruption, resentment, hate and anger. I could go on but the point is that all of these are the result of collective fear. ...And with that is the separation from the connection that I mentioned to you a few days ago."

Stevie looked at him, and for once the smile had evacuated its position. Stevie could not help but be affected and asked, "So what do we do to stop or negate this?"

Brightening up, Weishka said, "It is easy in concept. Each person on the planet must stay positive, stay connected… and trust. It is imperative they stay with love...Love and its attributes will hold fear at bay. Love will counteract any dark force."

Stevie *was* bewildered and for once said nothing.

"For now, Stevie, I suggest that you continue on your way and we will talk more on this later."

∞

As he walked a question kept burning into Stevie's mind that he had to ask, "Why did you not help me when that thing haunted me – I needed you?"

"You never need me, and if you go back you will learn that you don't need me or any guru. The Intelligence is in you, and you have the tools to intuit on your own, especially now with your new knowledge. Now to answer your question, I did not help because you needed to be the light on your own...Once you start to move towards the light, you go through the dark night of the soul…"

Weishka hesitated and searched for the easiest way to explain this important point. "Let me explain by way of a question or two. "Why do you keep your kitchen clean? You use all sorts of detergents and chemicals and you wipe and wash on a regular basis."

Stevie laughed to himself when he thought of his kitchen, cleaned less regularly than most, but answered, "To keep it clean."

Weishka wanted a deeper answer, "Yes, of course, but why do they have to be clean? Would it not save time if left dirty?"

Stevie knew the analogy was likely to be important and remained patient with the process. "Well, if not clean, germs will invade. Germs make us sick and kill us. The cleaning keeps them at bay. Is this the right answer?"

"Yes, it is. You see, if you look at dark force, the same as you would at those germs, there is a way to counteract them and that is by being positive, trust, be aware with love and joy. Love is the detergent, and joy the disinfectant.

This sounds easy and is easy, but humans make it hard because they forget. They lose their awareness." Slowing his voice even more for greater emphasis he said, "When you are aware it is impossible for any dark force to hurt you in any way. You will be completely safe and protected."

After saying this, Weishka was silent, leaving Stevie to his thoughts, where he found himself thinking for the second time in a short space of time; if only I knew all of this, my life would have been so different.

After the silence Weishka said, "You have another question, about the clash between the soul and the ego. You ready for it?"

"Yes, it is something that I have been pondering for some time. So please go ahead".

Weishka started his story by saying, "I call the man in this story Rodger. But really, the same applies to all. It will confirm what you realized about turning the ego on and off as you did. Perhaps sit down as it will take a few minutes.

Roger, newly born is without blemish. And at that age no fear disturbs him, nor does guilt or hate. He is open and positive with his main focus on food, warmth and being clean. When these are met and he is not asleep he has an inquisitive mind and wants to take in all that he can.

Also emerging in Roger are two energies. Sometimes these seem to oppose each other. The one is soft and gentle and often resides in the background. The other is loud and aggressive and tries to be prominent at all times. The first is called Soul, the second is Ego.

The influence on both Soul and Ego is impressed upon Roger's mind. The mind is passive in as much as it pretty much does as it is bid by Ego. But the mind does have a function and that is to retain memory, offering learning and reasoning power and supports the actions of the body. The mind is a bit like an old-fashioned switchboard that directs all incoming communication to connect and redirected to where things needs to go, and as such, it helps to build the personality. But the mind is really quite passive and easily influenced.

As a baby, the initial influence on Roger is not all that marked, and so the child is happy and without issues. However, Ego starts its work early to influence the child. Ego is ruthless and selfish in its desire to survive and will do anything to gain and retain control of Roger's mind. Its entire programming is to this end. It does this in many ways, such as trying to move the mind from love to fear, because when within fear rationality goes haywire. And when in fear Ego has complete control. Another way Ego divides and rules is through convincing the mind, or the personality, that it is not good enough, that it has inadequacies and that things will always turn out badly, and so Roger, via his mind, has self-esteem issues. The ego is also pretty good at doing things like having to justify its self to make it look better. It does this so well that often we get in a huff to express our self-perceived superiority in a discussion or an argument. For instance, later when Roger is older, often times he will have to be right and may say or do almost anything to prove that to the other person.

Soul, on the other hand would try to teach the belief that he does not have to be right every time, and that there are times when it really does not matter. But as ego is pushy and at the forefront, and because Soul is gentler, and comfortably waits in the background. So of course, it is usually Ego who has its way, ensuring Roger's mind feels that it must be right, and damn it, it will be right, almost irrespective of the consequences.

At the age of four, Roger is more expressing his personality, which is a combination of his experiences and the way that he remembers these experiences, plus the results of Ego and Soul's influence. So, Roger is a mixture of ego and Soul influence, where one minute he is loving and gentle, stroking the cat, and another he is shouting for more ice cream, simply because this is a demand that he wants to make".

Stevie made the comment that that is how most children seem to be.

"Yes," replied Weishka, "anyway, at ten year old the influence on Roger is greater. He knows more and is seemingly more confident with the way that he is growing into the world. But underneath that there are self-esteem issues that he has difficulty coping with. Ego has done a wonderful job of instilling fear to make Roger feel uncertain in many aspects of his life, such as playing soccer or even being nice to his sister because he has allowed himself to be jealous of her – thinking that she is more loved by their parents than he is.

It was at this age that Soul said to Ego, "You know, as we are in this body of Roger's together, we should work together to make Roger a happier person. So, are you willing to work together?"

"Why would I want to work with you?" said ego, "As far as I'm concerned you can go to hell. Like this human, I have been given free will and I choose to go and do exactly as I please. You have no control or influence over me and I even resent the fact that you're talking to me."

Again Stevie interjected, "Sounds like my fear that came to visit me those times, doesn't it?"

Weishka just nodded and continued, "You may think that now, but you know that I have infinitely more power than you and that my power comes from a greater connection. You know that my power has come from the connection that created everything and that when this body of Rogers fails, I will be reabsorbed back into that power. Whereas your time here is limited."

"Listen to the rubbish. I have control of Roger, and as he gets older my control will be even greater. I will play him better than Mozart played the piano. I will play him at each stage of his life and at this young age it is easy to play him. All I have to do is suggest to his mind that he does not have as many toys as his friend Peter. Or I could suggest that his sister is given more things than Roger. And his mind listens and takes it all in."

"There is one big difference between you and I, and that is you are fear, where I am love. And you know that for this person to have the ultimate growth, which is his reason for being here, is to learn and understand that he must move from fear to love. And this will certainly happen and you know that it will happen."

Roger is now the young man trying to make his way in life. He currently has a desire to have a fancier car and flashy clothes. In quiet moments he knows that he cannot afford these, and sometimes can't understand why he feels that he needs them. But if one could look into Roger's body at that time, Ego could be seen slouching against a wall with a smug grin on his face. Ego knew where this unreasonable desire stems from.

Although he can't afford it, Roger goes to the bank and borrows the money. He almost convinced himself, as he did the bank manager, as to how he would be able pay off the car.

But also, in those quite moments Roger felt that something was missing. He did not know what this was but felt a strong pull in another direction. It felt like he was a leaf on a stream and that the stream was ever flowing in a specific direction. This unknown feeling kept suggesting to him that all he had to do is to let go and float the way with the current and all would be right. But Ego explicitly would not allow that to happen and so the leaf would get caught up on logs and rocks, and stuck in eddies.

There were times in drunken conversations at bars and parties that people spoke about a better way, a spiritual way, way that is softer and gentler. Where fear was put aside and love was embraced. And when in these conversations he knew instinctively that what was said was correct. But none, it seemed, knew how to attain it, and of course the feeling would go when someone shouted out, "Whose round is it?" Once again it was Ego who was lurking in the background ever vigilant to stamp out any insurrection.

Soul asked Ego, "What do you get from keeping Roger in the place of fear?"

"I told you before I get control."

"But why do you need control, what are you scared of losing?"

This resonated with Stevie who listened with interest.

"There was silence from Ego.

At thirty Roger has two children of his own, a beautiful girl and a lovely little boy. He loves his children but is torn because he no longer loves their mother. It is Ego, who in the background pulls the strings to ensure that the dislike of his wife grows. It seems that they have a massive fight once a week, doors would slam, voices are raised and insults thrown. If only I could get out of debt thinks Roger, then it would not be so hard on either of us. We would not have to work as hard and perhaps we could get a nanny to help with the children. Damn it, life is just too busy.

Ego calls out to Soul and says "Hey you, see how easy it is for me to manipulate Roger? I'll always have the power to do as I choose with this human."

Soul smiles a gentle smile, but says nothing.

"Has the cat got your tongue," asked Ego. "Nothing to say? You claim that you come from a superior energy, how does that energy support you and Roger when I have complete control over him?"

Soul, in a gentle voice said, "It's true that you control Roger, he is fearful, in debt and has very low self-confidence (just like me Stevie thought). He is argumentative because you have made him of low self-worth. But he and you have free will and so that he will grow or decline according to his own will. I will not interfere. But I will always be here as a soft and gentle influence, one where, as he likens in his own mind, as being a leaf on an ever-flowing current moving towards a life of deeper meaning. You know that what he is referring to, as the leaf, is where he moves from a state of fear, to one of love. At any time in his life he can move from the fear that you effect on him to the love that is his birthright.

From Fear To Love is a Spiritual Journey offering the choices that he makes throughout his life to become the person who he should be. Offering understanding about the fear that blocks his path to inner peace and denies him his love. It opens a spiritual path, encouraging him to follow a journey that gives freedom from the tyranny of fear so that he can grow."

Stevie interjected, "Sounds awfully like me".

"Ego did not bother to answer and wandered off without a care in the world. But Soul called out after him, "You have kept this man small

enough for long enough and it is time you released your grip on him."
But ego just kept walking away.

Perhaps because of his difficult situation, or perhaps to try and get some sense back into his life, Roger started to allow himself to float down the stream with the leaf. It felt good. In fact, it felt better than good – it felt natural and how it should be. Supporting this, he gained some friends who were following this path. They recommended books and so with guidance and what he learned from the books, he started to get a better understanding as to how he was in fear and not love. All he had to do was to compare those friends with himself and he could see that they had lives that flowed better, and that seemed to work in a way that gave them a satisfying life. They seemed calmer and more compassionate. They spoke of love and often seem to be of love.

But his life was hard with the debt, and long hours at work. And then the coming home to his wife, who seemed to hate him. Seemingly, the only value were his children, so natural, so unencumbered – was I ever like that he wondered?

At forty, Roger was sleeping on the couch and not in the main bedroom with his wife.

Ego laughed in the background. Roger thought, why am I sleeping on the couch? The thought depressed him. It suddenly struck him that right now, in this sad state how insidious fear is. I have these feelings and don't even notice. I need to be able to change this and be more positive – at all times."

Stevie shuddered.

It was then that Soul said to Ego, "In time he will wake up from the sleep, and you will not have the hold on him. When he embraces Love we will see a mind content in harmony with its world and the greater Universe".

Weishka asked, "You following the story okay?"

"Sure am, you can continue."

"Roger and he is holding a glass of wine in his hand. He took a minute to leave the party to go outside for reflection. It was his fifty-fifth birthday party and he was trying to make sense of his life. He was just starting to get out of debt when he finally left his wife. He was bitter about the thought of the 50% of their assets that he left her with. His children were now grown up and loved and treated him with respect. But even better, they both have children and so these grandchildren gave him a different perspective on life. He does not care how much time he missed out on, he would never sacrifice his time away from them. He realized that they gave him perspective and taught him a better way to value life.

Although his life was still difficult, he pursued the leaf as it pulled towards a calming influence. He was not as panicked as he was and was calmer and happier. And although he did not really understand it, he was moving from fear to love. Even though, he still had a long way to go, Ego doubled its efforts to retain control. Recently he was able to nip in the bud an insurrection that Roger was planning, whereby he was to spend more time in quietness, listening to Soul. Ego reminded Roger of the debt that he was in, and of that payment that he had to make in a few weeks' time. Of course, Roger panicked and stayed longer at work to try and earn that extra commission.

Ten years later Roger was a happier person. He knew that the floating leaf showed the way and since he had spent more time pursuing it, his life was much better. Behind the scenes, and unbeknownst to Roger's mind, Soul and Ego had another conversation. It was Ego who was saying, "You, with your love may have gained ground over Roger but I still have ultimate control. Yes, I admit that my control is not as strong as it was but I still do have control. For instance, Roger is still scared to trust his new girlfriend Bianca, even though it is obvious that she loves him and wants only the best for him. It is easy for me to suggest to Roger's mind, just remember what happened with Julie, and that they are all like that, and that you will never satisfy any of them, and that they are all going to end up taking your assets, and that she's only there whilst it suits her."

Soul in its gentle voice said to Ego, "I am with love, I am calm, I give compassion to the mind. You create the opposite, you disrupt, unsettle and create nervousness. You know that it would be in your interest to back off a bit, as the mind will be happier and the body healthier, meaning the body will live longer and give you a longer life."

"Fool you", said Ego. "Do you think I worry about the peace of mind of this person? I have one desire, and that is to be prominent in all that this person thinks and does."

Not ruffled, Soul continued, "I also allow the mind free will to choose who or what it listens to, and so it is up to mind if it lets you influence it. By nature, I am more powerful than you, and therefore I have no fear of you, but the human does.

Ego responded with, "If I let you be in charge, I would almost be dead, that is how pathetic you are. You think that I am evil. I just want what I want."

Soul said, "No, you are not evil, just misguided."

"Look here Soul, his body must have clothes, food, drink, and sleep, and be led. I do the leading, and direct him. What is wrong with that?"

"Ego, perhaps one day you will understand that when a human is at the point of love, as opposed to that of fear, that they have achieved their specific purpose for their life. This is the divine instinct, which all humans naturally respond to."

"Who cares", replied Ego.

"When I talk of fear, you Ego, are a classic example. Your whole purpose is to retain control because otherwise you 'fear' that without the control you will be diminished. This is true, but you cannot see otherwise. In fact, you are more fearful than the human".

"I am not in fear," said ego angrily, and quickly removed himself from this line of conversation.

In the last days of Roger's life he was the happiest that he has ever been. His children with him, as well as his grandchildren, he felt nothing but love for them. He is glad that his life is ending this way, and knows that this is how it should be.

Soul interrupted Ego's worries, "I thank you Ego for the role that you played in Roger's life. You taught him what love is through knowing what fear is, and thereby you have inadvertently taught him to move from fear to love.

Do you remember when Roger was just ten years of age, you and I had a conversation where I said that I have the energy of a greater power than you do. You scoffed at what I said. But do you not understand now that I allowed you to continue with your role of disruption and sewing fear so that the human could understand what love really was as a result of having lived in fear? And you have seen it in this last quarter of his life where he lived mostly in love and moved from fear. So, I have much to thank you for the role that you have played, even if unwittingly."

Ego was frantic with worry as it knew that Roger's body was about to end, and with it would be the end of ego. Ego was afraid because it did not know what would happen to him once he lost consciousness as a result of death. He fought his panic at the thought of not having an existence, of not being able to have an influence within a life. At times it wondered what the purpose of his existence was for. In fact, he had wondered this for most of his life but because he did not have an answer that satisfied his worry, he focused even harder on maintaining control of Roger's mind. He had to, he had no choice as it could only be through control that he felt he could cling to something. But at this late juncture of his existence he now wonders if he was not foolish with that belief. He sighs, and knows that he has lived an entire life and still does not have the answer. Perhaps that soft fool Soul knows better. What if he is right? How would Roger's life be if I did not exert such negative influences on it? What if I allow Roger's mind to move more from fear to love? Oh, this is idiotic, I'm just scared because I'm about to expire and I do not know what that really means.

Roger knows he is about to go. He pities some of those other people in the aged care facility who are bitter about life and regret much about it. But being so full of love as Roger is, he does not let this affect him.

He knew at the age of around forty he had to step upon a path to find what eluded him all his life. At that time, he yearned for the feeling of calm and serenity, the feeling that he felt he deserve to honor himself and step outside his self-imposed darkness, believing that he was unlovable.

And later, he finally stepped in the sunshine of his freedom. To truly know what it is like to feel like a free man, worthy of his own faith and love.

With him, at his bedside were his children, and his wife Bianca, almost his last words to them was, "Our reality is a byproduct of our thoughts, or more particularly, an effect created by our thoughts, where our thoughts are the cause of this effect. This conforms to the most fundamental law in nature, being cause and effect. We can see the effects of our thoughts throughout our life and when you change the cause you create a different effect.

Our journey is to look past the body that holds the crucible of our life and search for the essence of our self. To look inside our heart and find the inner passage, which leads to the door that holds all our secrets. Behind this door there are two other doors and each will need to be opened. One will open the self to sunshine and all that is good within the human spirit for it is our mind of love.

The other door is where our demons are stored, our nightmares of guilt and suffering. Where our fears that torment and pillage our mind from rest and contentment. Make no mistake, this is the door that holds all our darkness and foreboding and are the obstacle that hinders our progress along our path to spiritual freedom. This room of darkness is the home of our frightened self. It was my house that housed all my pain and suffering, sadness, and insecurities. This is the mind of fear. It was from this place that I moved from to the door of love.

Rodger had to stop and rest a while. His family urged him to remain quiet and rest but he would have nothing of it, and in what seemed to be his last moments continued; it is imperative that you move out of your fear and into love, and by doing so you will find …

It was at this moment that Ego collapsed as Roger's love merged into the greater energies, Ego became dust and was scattered in the winds.

Soul smiled at the successful conclusion of Roger's life. It could have been easier on Roger if he followed the leaf years earlier. But with free will, what will be will be.

∞

Stevie did not want to comment on the story. He wanted to think about it first and so said, "Wow, you are some story teller".

Weishka knew Stevie was avoiding the issue but was happy enough to give him the space and so said, "Well, all our history has been passed down through stories, as was our learning. But this is not a handed down story, I created it for you as I felt you could relate to it.

∞

"Okay what is love?"

"Love is many things, it is awareness, for without awareness you are likely to slip into negativity. And yes, positivity is love, negativity is darkness. Remembering who you are is another aspect of love.

Love starts with loving yourself. Self-love is the well from which springs external love. The Intelligence is intelligent because it is made of love and you are made from the same substance and so the love is within you. It is wisdom, joy, respect, peace, trust, compassion, belief in the oneness of all, and gratitude. When you live with these principles you live with love. It should be easy to see that if you do not embody yourself with these qualities then that is when your life breaks down. It is for this reason that I said earlier that love is the most powerful force there is.

By employing those traits that make up love you set off metaphysical events. It is the metaphysical component of all creation. Ego, as the last story shows diminishes love as its own importance will try and usurp love. The more time put into absorbing these traits, the stronger your love will be, and as a metaphysical force, the more it will protect you. But it does not only end with you. Your love has an energy that also has the power to protect all people and your planet. It is like a light, it does not only shine to show you the way, it lights everyone's path. Love is your gift from The Intelligence and it can be your gift to humanity."

Weishka disappeared to let Stevie think about this. Stevie kept walking and let his thoughts slow down and soon felt calm, his mind floating in nothingness. This went for some time and he was amazed when he heard the words, loud and clear: "Take a close look at me, for I am what you are!" That was it, no more. He knew that the voice that said these words was not Weishka's – then who's?

"Who are you?" He thought, "come back, are you there? Please come back" He did not really need to ask from where the message came

– this was clear. Of course, there was silence and he was left to ponder what had been fed to him.

There were times when he had heard references in the Bible and other spiritual writings with the same or similar words – "take a close look at me, for I am what you are, or I am that, etc.". But why would they be given without explanation?

The pondering lasted many minutes, but finally answers came. *"Take a close look at me, for I am what you are!"* came again:

I am the love, I am the gratitude, I am the wisdom, I am the awareness, I am compassion, I am the hopeful, I am what I want to become, I am the oneness. I am Jesus, I am Buddha, I am Muhammad and I am that I am.

Lastly; he found it interesting to consider the way the words were laid down; *"Take a close look at me, for I am what you are!"* They could have been; Take a close look at me, for you are what I am! This second meaning would seem to be one of 'superiority', as "you can be like me if you want". But the meaning as was given is humble, and is that not what we would expect? In fact, it suggests that it is what I am not what it is. That same thought again, I know what I am not, but not what I am, but now I'm given to believe that I am what The Intelligence is. He also marveled at the timing of this missive coming after the doing the 'Who am I' process. Before the process it would not have been as powerful.

∞

It was a beautiful night, warm and clear, without a breath of wind. The moon had not risen so the stars had the sky to themselves. They were big and close, Stevie felt he could reach out and touch each one. He had made his burrow and eaten the roots and berries he gathered earlier. Some of these were the bulbs that the Bushmen had shown him. Whilst collecting wood he realized he was humming a song. It had been a long time since he had sung to himself.

He took out his fire-lighting equipment. It didn't matter that he was not as efficient as Weishka. But then this was his first attempt and the old man had probably done it thousands of times. Thirty minutes later he watched the flame that he had made – like Egyptian dancers against a black night danced and changed form. He remembered his Bushman friends, Bauxhau, Nxeu and the rest and laughed at the name they gave him – Lxeua, Sideway Spear.

It wasn't long before the shimmering glowing embers worked their magic. His last conscious thought was – fire is good company when you are alone …

This time he found himself hovering over a massive landscape. It was one of desert and gums. The place teemed with animals; kangaroos and wallabies jumped with ease and power. Possums, the bushy-tailed cats of the gum tree gallivanted at night, where they preened and squabbled with a low-sounding growl. Light-pawed, they gracefully leapt from branch to branch, tree to tree. In the day they slumbered in tree stumps. Emu's, a flightless bird, roamed the terrain on long legs that powered them up to great speeds and for long periods at a time. With their tall necks they reach two metres high, the largest bird of this massive land. Resident for many thousands of years and perfectly adapted to the harsh and unpredictable conditions – they can go weeks without food and days without water.

There is an abundance of bird varieties, amongst the largest in the world, parakeets, galas, cockatoos and hundreds of others. At a later time, Stevie would think one can never be lonely in this bush because of the constant racket of warbles, tweets and all other manner of bird conversation. He was not sure of his favourite; the magpie with its lyrical and changing parley or the Kookaburra with its laugh of "aaaaaAhooaaaaaKKkoooAAhooo" that could be heard a kilometre away. At first its raucous shrills sent a chill up his spine.

It is an old land and so are its people. Some say 68,000 years of continuous habitation – a hardy race that knows the land, a race that has formed strong spiritual connection from observation and experience. The name that would have been used by their forebears is Koori but of late they are called Aboriginals, but irrespective, they are the First people of this large island.

In this land that Stevie found himself, it was not as an inhabitant but an observer. The land is now called Australia. It was part of the great

Gondwana Land that was attached to Asia and encompassed most of the land mass of the Southern Hemisphere. For scientists, Gondwana Land is of interest because of the spread of organisms across the land bridges. For anthropologists, the interest is the flow of humanity from its roots in Southern Africa. For Stevie, he was fascinated because most of the spiritual practices taught here were the same as the Native American Indian and the Bushmen of the Kalahari but he was only to learn this later.

As he hovered and soared across an inland sea as vast as the United Kingdom, he heard the telepathic voice of his mentor, "Amazing, isn't it?" Stevie looked around and smiled and heard the thought, "Didn't think you were going to have this all on your own, did you?"

They headed inland, but as the area was so vast it could have been anywhere. Nor did they have any idea as to when in time this was. They descended to observe a group of the hardy inhabitants. A ritual meeting was in progress. Both Stevie and Weishka settled in the branches of an Iron bark gum to observe.

The group contained three adolescents and four elder members of the tribe. One was a 'Mooroops', a man of spiritual connection. It was the Mooroops who was talking and paused in conversation as he felt a new vibration. Looking up in the tree he saw Weishka and Stevie. Recognizing Weishka as a fellow shaman, he nodded a welcome greeting. The six were watching the Mooroops and followed his gaze but only saw the overhanging tree with a dark blue-sky background. They knew the Mooroops could see things they couldn't.

Whilst this interaction was going on, Stevie was fascinated to see a Dingo (wild dog) at the feet of the Mooroops. The dingo also looked up and could see or sense Weishka. It gave a non-aggressive growl. The ears seemed to be permanently erect, giving it an intelligent look. It was ginger-coloured with a white chest. He noticed that the teeth were much larger than normal dogs and remembered reading somewhere that the Dingo is the largest meat-eating mammal in Australia. They followed the early human migration from Asia across the land bridge many thousands of years earlier.

The Mooroops continued with the discussion. "Bora is the time when a boy becomes man, it is a time when your connection to the land is made and your responsibility to the land is felt. For this final act towards your initiation as an adult of the land, you will journey (walkabout). This may take many days, weeks or months. It is better if you start off together but separate after four days. If you cross paths in the mulga (a tree and also the bush) that is fine."

Stevie was aware of the similarities of the Bora and his journey of learning. He would follow this with interest. Looking closer, one of the boys seemed to be familiar but he dismissed the thought. The Mooroops was a small man and carried a face of wisdom. It was a happy face and full of understanding. He continued, "Before you were born your spirit existed in the form of an animal, a plant or as an ancestral spirit and so as you go in search of manhood you search for your spirit. When you do this with intent, your story of the land is revealed. History is never far as it lives in the land; it is your task to find that history. You will live off the land and respect all creatures, plants, shrubs and ancestor rocks. Listen to them, they will guide you. You will follow the song lines (Dreaming tracks) of our ancestors by chanting the songs and hearing the call of the spirits. By singing you will bring the spirits and the land together, while finding the way of manhood. As part of your Bora, you have been taught chanting and things mystical. To go beyond the five senses where you enter The Dreamtime (time before conscious thought) and hear stories as told by the Ancestors. It is a time of solitude and reflection, and if you listen you will hear stories that come from our old culture."

∞

As they left, the skin-family (a term that loosely refers to the collective of the tribe as family. Family to the Australian Aborigine is central to life) were all were there to wave them off and offer last-minute advice.

Aminya and Piltapari spent most of the time together. Both were excited because of the pending lessons and journey. A journey that they knew would not only be of the foot but also of the mind. They knew that they should be solemn and respectful, but with the exuberance of youth they felt invincible and euphoric. Coolah was more of a loner and usually walked on his own.

It was Coolah who Stevie was drawn to. Stevie looked to Weishka as he was going to ask why he was drawn to Coolah, but he was in silent conversation with the Mooroops.

∞

The first three days may have been carefree but they were important days to ease them into the land. The land seemed to enter into the Bora as it supported them by offering plenty of game to hunt and consume.

It was on the fourth day, with the sun frying the land and all on it that they sought some shade. Seeing a solitary tree that was far towards the horizon they headed to it. Piltapari and Aminya chatted, and said that it would take them about an hour, but after much walking, the tree did not seem any closer. "Must be a massive tree," said Aminya. It was, as they saw when they finally reached its deep welcoming coolness. But long before reaching it, they could feel an energy.

Piltapari said to the others, "Are you feeling it? It gets stronger as we get closer?"

Aminya nodded, whilst Coolah stopped because he was afraid. "Don't be afraid," the other two said, "this is good energy. It is powerful energy."

Standing under the tree, it felt like a thousand bees buzzing. Yet there were no bees. "The energy, she is strong," whispered Aminya, "and it is female energy."

Piltapari knew that Aboriginal law deemed it necessary that the woman leave the skin clan when about to give birth. Sometimes it is close by. For others it takes many days. Always the place is kept secret from the community.

"What is it?" asked a frightened Coolah.

"I think a birthing tree," answered Piltapari. They are used for special births and gives the baby the power of the tree. See how big the tree is? See this hole in the tree, the Mooroops burn out this hole. It is big enough for the mother and several female attendants. One of the attendants always carried the power of the Ancestors.

The others looked around and took in the size of the base of the tree. Indeed, Piltapari was right, it could fit several people. Piltapari was stunned to hear a voice in his head. "Did you hear that?" he asked the others.

"What?"

Coolah's eyes had fright in them. He started to mumble something…

"Shoosh," hissed Piltapari, "listen".

"I am tree, and I offer protection to all that seek me. There are times when a chosen one comes to enter the world from my roots. I bestow my Sky-Earth energy into the child. You, Piltapari, are one of the chosen ones."

"What do you mean, 'chosen one'?" asked Piltapari.

"It is one who carries the spirit of the ancestors to help show the way. You were born within my womb, protected by my sanctity. It is your time and I called you to come home to me, to feel my energy. This is in you, and of you. You carry me wherever you travel. Some are born in caves as Earth-Womb offers another power type. But you are of Earth-Sky energy."

All his life Piltapari had felt a stronger connection to the callings of the ancestors than his friends. He never said anything as he did not want to seem different from them. Now he knew he was.

The tree continued, "It is your time to come into your power, to use it to help others."

"How do I use your power?" he asked.

"It is not my power, it is ancestral power. I only help in making you feel it. Now you know it, call upon it. All it requires is to stop and listen. They will speak… You will hear."

Heading towards the tree, Aminya said, "I am going to climb the tree."

"No," shouted Piltapari, louder than was necessary, "don't climb, it is sacred."

Piltapari was told that men don't normally go to a birthing tree, but he needed to be told things and that is why the call from the tree was strong. Piltapari saw himself as a baby under the tree. Later his mother carried him home. One of the helpers also carried something in the bark of the tree. When arriving back into the community, there was a ceremony, whilst they buried his placenta and the bark in the ground. Piltapari was told, "This ensured you became part of the dreaming."

Piltapari remembered the teachings from the Elders from when he was little. Dreamtime energy gave us the trees. Trees stand tall and touch Father Sky. Its feet reach deep into Mother Earth. Tree connects both and is neither air like sky or solid like earth and rock. Tree was given to us to use. We use the bark and sticks to make a moortangi (a hut). Trees give us medicine and shade in hot weather, and fire to warm us when cold. We also make fire for cooking. Trees, like us, live in communities. It is their tribe. If a tree is moved and replaced elsewhere it has to be sung into the ground.

But this tree is not in a community, it stands alone and tall, thought Piltapari.

∞

After leaving the tree, they continued until they came to a water hole. Even though it was more mud than water, they followed the cultural ritual of picking up a handful of dirt and throwing it into the water to introduce themselves. It was here that they parted.

Aminya had a calling to travel towards the far hills, which from that distance looked like an ant on the flat. It was in this direction that he headed. Piltapari watched his friend depart. Aminya means the Quiet One and his name serves him well, Piltapari thought.

Piltapari continued toward the sun. He did not know why but felt a calling to go that way.

Coolah was sullen and sat by the mud hole. This attitude was normal to him. His birth name was Oogee, which means headdress, given as a result of the unusual tufts of hair that he was born with. But over time, he became known as Coolah, the Angry One.

Stevie was given a scene of Oogee as a child and scanned his energy field. It was healthy and vibrant. But now Coolah's was small and dark. It had a menace about it, like a cyclone front.

∞

Stevie and Weishka followed Piltapari as he wandered the vast desert, where mirages shimmered with heat that scorched as if standing too close to a fire. Most of the terrain was flat and dusty. The land colour depended on the time of day. If evening, it was a golden desert. Through the day it was a harsh reddish-brown, which was stark against the strong blue of the clear sky. There had been drought and many of the animals had died or departed. It was hard to find food, but Piltapari was well-taught and able to survive on the ground roots he dug.

∞

In Piltapari's meditations and discussions with the ancestors he was shown many things. But there was a vision that scared Piltapari. It was where they showed him 'Myndie', the mythical snake. He saw Myndie kill its brother. But snakes do not travel together he thought. And if they do come across each other they keep a wary distance. He wondered what it meant and was disturbed by an image of the snake's face as it glared at him, as if he was the next victim.

∞

Aminya had lived on the mountain for several weeks. Sitting high on the headland as he often did, he looked over the plains far below. He was self-sufficient when on his own, with enough to eat and had found water without problem. And he enjoyed the solitude, which allowed him to consider his role in life. He knew that he had the connection to spirit but had no want to be a Mooroops. This was his friend Pilapari's path, not his. He knew that he was wise and many regarded his soft-spoken countenance with wisdom. But he wanted children, lots of them. He smiled as he remembered the girl who was to give them to him. They had not spoken about this as it was forbidden until he reached manhood. But both he and Moolawa (Daylight) knew it to be so. They had always known.

As the days passed, he became more and more with the land, sharing the same mind. The elders had been trying to show him this from the time he was little. With one mind he knew where the water was, even though he had never been to this area before. The same with food; he would be walking and the shared mind would whisper, "There is a tortoise behind this large rock." And sure enough there was one. For his part Aminya thanked the land for the support and cooked the tortoise with glee as he liked its meat.

The shared mind tried to tell him to be careful and that he must watch his back. This was a strange message, and for once passed it off without another thought.

∞

Coolah sat by the water hole for three days, too lazy to move. Besides, he thought, if the ancestors want to talk to me, they can come to me. He managed to hit a dove with a stone. It was the only animal that had come to the mud. Its flesh did not offer much to satisfy his hunger. He brooded over the friendship that Aminya and Piltapari shared. They have always been like that, excluding him. One day I will show you, he thought, especially you, Piltapari. You think you are so much with spirit. You watch, you'll see.

Stevie kept scanning Coolah's aura and was concerned. For some reason he felt a kindred spirit to him. Then he realized that what Coolah was feeling was the same anger he felt with Joe and Doris. This was an incredible revelation to see another with the same hate and aggression to life and other people.

∞

After many weeks on the mountain Aminya felt it was time to come down to the flat. He did so, and was encouraged to follow a song line towards the north. By now he had trusted all the callings and knew that it was correct to follow.

∞

Piltapari had had a hard time on his walkabout. He connected to the land and the ancestors and was one with them. But the ancestors kept setting traps and testing him. Although difficult, Piltapari has a strong will and understood that as a potential Mooroops his lessons would be harder than those of the others and that he must always remain clear of thought. He limped along using a stick to support himself. He had been bitten by a black snake. Their bite is not lethal unless the victim is old and weak, but the poison is strong. As the snake flashed and struck, Piltapari remembered the image of Myndie, the mythical snake. He wondered if the image foretold of this snake bite or if there was more that was to come.

∞

Hunger forced Coolah away from the water hole. With anger in his heart he wandered aimlessly. He could not understand why he could not easily find food or water. He survived by eating roots. They were easy to find but tasted bitter and made him shudder each time he chewed one. But until his luck turned, he would have to keep on eating them.

He had lost all track of time. Days and weeks swam through his mind, but he reasoned that it must have been a long time because the sun set earlier and woke up later. Nor was its bite as strong. Feeling that he had adequately suffered and that enough time had passed, he headed back towards the skin clan and was confident that Manhood would be bestowed on him.

It was then he crossed the path that Aminya had taken whilst going to the north, and so followed it. It did not take long before he caught up with him. But instead of calling a greeting before entering the camp as custom dictates, he crept closer, like a dog sniffing for morsels. He saw Aminya kill a small goanna (lizard). Delirious with hunger, Coolah sprang out and tried to wrestle the goanna away from Aminya. In the struggle, Coolah picked up a rock, the same size as an emu egg, and struck Aminya across the temple. As he did, everything froze, caught in time, Aminya's eyes were wide open in surprise. His grip on the lizard softened, and as if in slow motion, reeled back, and folded into the dust. His staring eyes saw no more.

Coolah knew that he had killed Aminya but did not care. He cooked and ate the goanna meat.

Stevie, powerless to intervene, watched in horror as the tragedy unfolded.

∞

That same afternoon Piltapari felt darkness. Whatever it was, it was thick and heavy. He had been limping towards a community of trees. Suddenly his mind saw the snake. It struck with vengeance. Piltapari felt a sharp pain at his temple. He knew something bad had happened but did not know what. With concern he continued on his way as he tried to rub the pain from his temple.

∞

At the skin clan, the Mooroops had been skinning a possum that one of the children had killed, when he felt a pain and shuddered, as if hit with a rock on the side of the head. He saw an image of a flashing stone and staring eyes as the light went out of them.

∞

Even with all the tricks and traps set against him, Piltapari learnt well, he was pleased to have been chosen to be a Mooroops and that he must accept the responsibility. As he continued the journey, it became easier to receive information. By this time the ancestors were not just vague voices in his head; he could see and converse with them. In turn, the spirits were proud of Piltapari and knew that they had chosen well.

It was also time for Piltapari to return to the skin-clan. He knew his journey was over. He had also been called telepathically by the Mooroops. His spirit had visited him many times and welcomed him to the teachings. On this last occasion the Mooroops said, "Come, you have done well. It is time to return. But remember young one, the snake is still to strike. It has struck once and is ready to strike again."

Piltapari thought that when the Mooroops said, "It has struck once," he felt it was because of the snake bite he suffered. He wondered what the second strike would be.

∞

Piltapari estimated that with his bad leg, it would take nine or ten days to get back. At first his progress was slow, but after a time the poison reduced. The wound was like a melon that had burst in the hot sun. It was open and raw. He applied bark and herbs and gradually it improved.

He looked forward to his return to his skin clan as an adult – an equal.

∞

The Mooroops sent a message to Piltapari, "Careful!"

∞

Piltapari did not know what to make of it. Did this have something to do with the image he saw or another test?

∞

Coolah was sitting on a rocky outcrop watching the sun set. The ridge had been depleted of soil by wind and time. Out of the sun, a silhouetted image appeared. At first, he thought that he was hallucinating from hunger, but realized that it was Piltapari coming towards him. Hate filled mind. He had killed Aminya, and now he will kill Piltapari. With both of them dead, he would go back and pretend that he had not seen either of them after they separated. Crouching low he waited…

∞

Piltapari could feel evil. It was dark and thick as if he had walked into a wall of treacle. He knew danger was close – could be in those hills other there. But it would take days to go around it, it was so long.

∞

Stevie and Weishka watched with trepidation but could do nothing. Weishka held a calming hand on Stevie's shoulder.

∞

As Piltapari got closer to the clump of rocks he knew the evil of the snake was represented only a few metres in front of him. Cautiously, he entered a large crevice. The rock face, high on both sides was rough and red as if it had been stained by a millennium of sunsets. He could see that it was clear until the canyon turned a sharp corner. His heart pounded so much it felt like it was in his ears. "Look up!" his mind shouted, and as he did, he saw a figure drop a head-sized rock down on him. Piltapari was just fast enough to flatten himself against the cliff face, the rock grazing his arm as it fell harmlessly to the ground. No sooner did this happen, Coolah followed the rock down to land next to Piltapari. He had another rock in his hand – the same rock he used on Aminya.

So Coolah is the snake thought Piltapari as he prepared to defend himself. The thought was driven out of his mind as he struggled to fend off his attacker. Coolah fought like he was possessed, and when Piltapari got a glimpse of his face he could see he was. Coolah held a rock that he tried to use on Piltapari but Piltapari was able to shake it loose from his hand.

They rolled and tussled, blows were struck by both but weakened by the snake bite, Piltapari could feel himself tire. As he did, Coolah gained a position on top of Piltapari. Having a firm grip of Pilapari's hair, he lifted Pilapari's head to slam it back against the rock beneath. Coolah repeated this over and over again until there was no movement from his hated foe. Blood covered his hands and the surrounding rock. He stood up, elated. He knew he should feel remorse, but why? He had always wanted to hurt Piltapari. Now with both Piltapari and Aminya gone, he was the only one of his age group left and the clan were likely to treat him with more respect. He thought of hiding the body, but why worry as the dingoes would smell it and dispose of it quickly enough. In the Australian outback nothing is preserved.

He headed back, but went via the mud pond so he could wash off all traces of blood.

∞

The Mooroops felt the struggle and knew something bad had happened to Piltapari. He called his two sons, and together with the dingo, headed out. Every so often the Mooroops would stop, as if listening, and would adjust the direction. It took them several days to get to the body. In that time, they paused only briefly for food and rest.

The blood had dried and caked Piltapari head and the surrounding rock, but he was still alive, only just. He was lucky that the season was the colder one and that the canyon floor where he lay was mostly in shade.

The Mooroops took out the herbs that he had brought and sent his youngest son to collect more, for both the snake bite and the head wound. The other was to light a fire to smoke away the bad spirits.

As he administered the medicine, he called the spirits to help him bring Piltapari back to life.

∞

Three days later the Mooroops could feel Piltapari's life force getting stronger and knew that the danger had passed. But it was with anguish that he received the news that his eldest son had found the body of Aminya. Oooh no, Aminya, the Quiet One, he thought.

∞

The sons supplied a steady diet of meat and herbs that was made into a broth. They feed this to Piltapari. A week later Piltapari was strong enough to head back to the clan.

∞

Coolah had returned whilst Piltapari was recovering. He told the skin clan that after going on his own journey he saw no more of the others. He told a tale of mystical enlightenment and bravery, of how he had fought demons and overcome hardships on his way to confirming his manhood. The clan held reservations as they had seen Coolah grow up and knew he could be fanciful when it suited him. They waited for the Mooroops to return. When he did, it was with a grave countenance that he told of Aminya's murder and attempted murder of Piltapari. Piltapari was still sick and weak, the back of his head misshapen. But he would make a full recovery.

∞

The skin-family had been ruptured by the news of Coolah's acts and for many days the old people were undecided what to do. Tribal law states that murder must be met by death. But many felt that Coolah had been delirious with hunger. When the vote had been made, there were four votes each. It was decided to call on animal wisdom for clarity.

Early the next morning, long before the Sun was to rise the old people met. The animals would tell them what to do. They sat in a circle, all looking outward so the entire landscape could be watched. There was no talk, this was serious business. They knew it would not take long as sunrise is a late time for the animals, most had started their day long before.

"There, there up in the sky," said one old man. All turned in the direction and saw a Butcher Bird fly and land in a tree. Its message was clear. It had a grub in its beak. They watched as it impaled the grub on a dry branch.

The Mooroops nodded as did the rest. They must summons the Kurdaitcha, the ritual executioner – a bone pointer.

∞

The Kurdaitcha had arrived but stopped about fifty meters from the camp. At first no one noticed him as he had assumed a position of grace and meditation. He was standing upright, supported on one leg. The other was folded so that the sole of the foot pressed against the inside of his standing thigh. A hunting stick supported his balance, one end on the ground, the other resting in both hands. He was steady as a rock, his countenance inscrutable.

Dark, like granite, he had a deep curly black beard and firmly set brow line, which stared unyielding towards the skin group. Even at that distance, the eyes penetrated all who saw him.

Stevie marvelled at the strong and perfectly proportioned body – he was not young but appeared lithe and powerful. Naked, except for a skin belt, from which hung the lifeless body of several speared goannas.

This apparition could easily have just arrived from the dreamtime.

Without the slightest movement, he stayed there for half an hour. It was only then that he came over to confer with the Mooroops and some of the elders. Every so often they pointed to Coolah who was loosely tied to a tree. His glum face showing resentment at the proceedings.

One of the elders went to Coolah, untied him and bought him across to the gathering of the elders. The entire clan had come out to watch and stood in groups a little distance away. None spoke, all watched. For many, they have never seen the Kurdaitcha or an execution. As for Koori, it was a rare occasion when one is warranted. All eyes were on the Kurdaitcha as he unravelled something from a gum-bark cover. An "Ooooohaaa," came from the crowd as the Kuru (the death bone) was shown. It was a long shin bone of a human that had been sharpened at the end. Attached to it was the fur of an animal. To give the Kuru extra power, the Kurdaitcha had sung it (spoken spirit into it).

In a slow arching movement, the Kurdaitcha turned around whilst raising the Kuru. The turning continued until the Kuru pointed directly at Coolah. A soft chant had started deep within the Kurdaitcha then gained momentum. He was calling the spirits to come and take Coolah and teach him to be gentler in the next life.

Coolah's face was distorted in fear. His eyes bulged and mouth twisted, sweat poured from his face. He was frozen to the spot, powerless to run or hide.

It was Moolawa (Daylight), the girl who was to be Aminya's wife who went to Coolah.

Stevie shouted with amazement but the words, "That's Mandy," were not heard. For a moment Moolawa stood in front of Coolah. As she looked into his eyes, she said nothing but projected forgiveness. The sensitivity of the moment gave Coolah strength. He nodded, "Thank you." She gently steered him away from the clan, and then with a soft push on his back to indicate to him that he must now leave and go and make peace with his ancestors. The Kurdaitcha continued pointing the Kuru whilst chanting a soft chant that only he could hear or understand.

In a daze, Coolah stumbled away from the camp. He did not look back. The crowd did not move or take their eyes off the departing Coolah, until finally a dot on the horizon, merged into nothing.

∞

Stevie felt as if he was part of the clan and he found he was holding his breath. His eyes could not leave Moolawa until he whispered to Weishka, "Let's get out of here."

Weishka looked towards the Mooroops and nodded. The Mooroops nodded back as if to say, "Travel well brother shaman."

∞

Back, next to the fire that was burning as if no time had passed, Weishka said, "Auto suggestion… amazing how it plays a part in the belief structure." He said this to draw Stevie out of the depression that he descended.

At last Stevie responded, "Why kill him? Why did the council recommend death? I thought you were teaching me spiritual things.

This is no better than the old religions justifying death in the Inquisition or other times."

In a soft and gentle voice Weishka said, "Ritual execution as deemed necessary by the elders of the tribe is not for us to judge. I don't condone or condemn what happened. Fortunately, the use of ritual execution by a Kurdaitcha is seldom used. For the pointing of the bone to work the victim must be present to the ritual and aware of what is happening, because death is not likely to occur if the victim is unaware. The threat of having a bone pointed at one by a Kurdaitcha gives the expectation of death occurring sometime in the near future. It is the expectation that does the killing. There have been times when a bone had been pointed but the individual suffered no death because they did not believe in its power. So, Stevie, the power of the mind constructs and creates its own death. When a condemned person dies there are no obvious causes such as heart failure or a stab by a spear."

Weishka let Stevie take in what he had said until in a firmer voice Stevie said, "So, Weishka, what you are saying is that the Kurdaitcha's power is all in the mind of the condemned?"

"Yes."

"And what about the Kurdaitcha, does he really believe that he has the power to end another person's life through some sort of magic power?"

"In some cases, yes, they do. But does it matter as they know the condemned believe it and so they know how powerful the process is. In some cases, they know that the energy that they transmute though the Kuru and their chanting is enough to change the brain waves or vibration to one of extreme negativity. The victim's own mind takes over to cause the actual death. Stevie, the reason I took you there was to show you the power of the mind to be either a friend or an enemy.

But there is another thing that you must understand, and that is the power of family within their community – the skin clan and belonging is so important to each and every member. Without it, they would die out, although they do not use that word, they prefer passing on. So, in Coolah's case, he is condemned to leave the skin clan, and that is as good as death."

"I understand, but why was Mandy there?"

"It was one of her past lives and it helped to show you again of our development over many lifetimes."

∞

After Weishka had gone, Stevie stared into the fire. He had learnt so much over the course of the journey, but what he had learnt on this night was probably the most powerful. He could see from this lesson how unresolved anger can destroy, as it did Coolah. He considered his life and could see how anger had grooved his mind into a way of thinking, and therefore a way of being.

He rolled into his burrow and thought of the land that he had just returned from. A magical land of strange animals and wise people, entwined with the elements and seasons, of Dreamtime, Song lines and spirits, of a girl called Moolawa who…

EMERGENCY ROOM …
SUNDAY 5:03 PM

Rose reported for work an hour early and went straight to Stevie's bed. She was relieved to see that he was still there. Quickly scanning the chart, she hoped to see an improvement – no improvement. She dreaded the time when Dr Ritchie came on shift.

Although the chart had the name Steven Jardine, she automatically thought, "Come on, Stevie, you have one hour."

Walking out, she noticed the girl sitting in the corner and so veered over to her. "Can't be easy for you waiting like this?"

Mandy looked up and saw the nurse who seemed to do a lot of hovering around Stevie's bed sad-smiling at her. But before she could say anything the nurse asked, "Coffee? Let's get out of here for a while."

To get to the cafeteria they had to cross a garden courtyard. Winter mist shrouded the air, dark-bellied clouds hovered just above the tree line. Halfway across, Mandy's phone rang. It was one of her friends who had been supporting Mandy in this process. She mouthed to Rose, "Sorry, won't be long."

Mandy stopped and spoke into the phone, oblivious to the cold and drizzle. Rose stood under the entrance overhang and waited patiently. As she did, she observed Mandy — stylishly dressed with a mauve jacket and a light blue scarf, the pastels fitting her natural gracefulness. Watching Mandy, Rose wondered if the light had gone out of her eyes.

When seated at a corner table in the cafeteria both cupped their hands around their coffee and waited for the other to speak. Mandy wondered why the nurse asked her to come along. The cafeteria was plastic, red and yellow, like egg yoke covered in tomato sauce. Not an inspiring place but it was quiet.

Rose felt a kinship with Mandy, probably because of the fact that her William and Steven would have been of a similar age. Whilst staring at the egg and tomato sauce tablecloth, she finally broke the silence, "There are many things in life that we can't explain." Not a profound comment, but it started the conversation.

"Yes, I guess you're right. Sometimes there seemed to be more ups than downs. I can't explain why Stevie did what he did… but… there is one thing, but I don't want to talk about it."

"That's okay, I don't want to pry, nor do I want to burden you with my problems, but I feel drawn to you. Can I tell you why?"

Mandy looked at Rose and could see in her eyes a need to talk, and thought, might as well listen as somehow, I need to lift myself out of my depression. "Please tell me if you think it will help in some way."

Rose nodded her head in thanks but had difficulty starting… twenty, then thirty seconds passed. When it came out, it was fast. "My son William died twenty-six months ago. He was about the same age as Steven. Each time I look at Steven, I see William."

With red and swollen eyes, Rose continued, "It makes me so sad. I am sorry that I tell you this but I can't help myself." She stopped talking whilst she unravelled a used tissue, her face red and splotchy from the tears. Mandy, offered her a new one and took another for herself.

"I'm sorry to hear that, and don't know why but I am glad you told me. I think you're reaching out to me like you have can help us both… How did he die?"

Rose blew her nose before the answer came, "Motorbike accident… I hated that bike."

But what Rose did not mention was that William had been drinking all morning in the kitchen. Rose became annoyed and moaned at him, "You'll never amount to anything if you continue the way you're going. Just like your father, a life wasted".

William, staggered to his feet, and without saying a word, guzzled the last of the beer in the bottle, picked up his helmet and walked out the door. An hour later Rose received the phone call that told her son was dead. Rose blames herself for William's death.

They were quiet, each buried under the weight of their own thoughts, until with a half-hearted laugh Mandy reminded Rose that they had forgotten their coffee. Both drank in silence until Mandy blurted out, "Stevie has had a really difficult life. In fact, there are many things he just wouldn't talk about. He's such a clam that I have not been able to open up. He is a wonderful person, always has been. We met when we were children… it's funny but it was as if I had known him all my life… he came at a time when I was so unsure of myself. Everything in my life was really good. My parents were loving and attentive, I was good at sport and school work, but something seemed to be missing. Whatever it was it made me miserable. And even at that young age Stevie had the ability to say the right things. He never judged me and only saw the best in me… … I have much to thank him for.

After my university studies I went on a six-month vac of Europe. In Bulgaria one Saturday night I was separated from my friends in a town square. Four young men, farmers, dragged me into their van and repeatedly raped me… … for several years I was a broken person, but when Stevie and I re connected it was he who convinced me that I had so much to live for. Yet, look at what he has done. Often, we can help others but when it comes to our own issues… The thought was not finished, it floated heavily in the air.

More silence, each second a stab of pain as both mourned, but then Mandy continued, "I have to tell you something, I have not told anyone other than Stevie." She took a deep breath as if to fortify herself for what was about to come. "Stevie and I broke up eighteen months ago. At the time I was pregnant with his child, but I didn't know it. After learning of my pregnancy, I tried to contact him, but my messages were ignored. I was distraught and did not want my baby to come to life without happiness. I felt that the baby would know there was sadness and would interpret it as not being wanted. I was also angry at Stevie for the way he broke it off. I won't go into that, but I made the decision to have an abortion… … you have to understand that I was so emotional and not thinking straight… two weeks later the foetus was gone… and with it my soul… I wrote Stevie an angry letter… blaming him… called him immature. I have only loved two people in my life, one is Stevie, and the other was my baby…. Well, that's not strictly true, my parents were wonderful, but you know what I mean. But coming from a loving family as I was lucky enough to have come from, I cannot understand my irrational decision to abort. It is so out of my character."

Not being able to go on, she stared out the window, not seeing the rain-sodden garden and car park beyond.

Rose knew that she must keep quiet until Mandy was strong enough to continue. When she did her voice held no life, her lips pursed, her eyes were looking towards the floor, "And now they're both gone."

"Mandy" Rose said, "you can't blame yourself. You did say that his life had been difficult."

"Yes, but when Stevie received that letter, it would have been the straw that broke the camel's back. It's my fault that he's in there dying."

"Mandy, we can't change the past, I can't bring back William, but we can pray that Stevie pulls through. We must not give up hope. He is not doing well… we need a miracle"

Mandy nodded – unconvinced.

After a time, Rose stood up and said, "I must get back."

Mandy also stood and said, "I'll come with you to continue my vigil."

Rose asked, "Do you have friends who can help you through this. On your own it is too hard… I know. You have to take care of yourself… or you will break down."

"I'm okay, I have dozens of friends, who are constantly calling or texting. But in terms of getting through this, I will be positive… be strong, and will hold off any break down until it's all over… one way or another… Then… ."

As they were strolling out, and back to the ward, Mandy said, "Thanks Rose, somehow I feel a bit better."

Rose stopped and faced Mandy. Mandy could not help but grab Rose and hug her. They came together, each taking strength from the other.

∞

"Today I am going to have the day off and enjoy this spot," Stevie announced to no one in particular. The afternoon before he had found the lake and decided to camp there. The lake was wide and joined steep tree-covered hills around three sides – it was alpine-like. The contrast of the green foliage and the water was lovely on the eye. He chose the flat side to camp. It was perfect as there was a cluster of trees to give shade and shelter.

Most of the morning he swam and lay in the sun. By mid-afternoon he was feeling languid and decided to sit and lean against one of the trees. At first, he looked at the branches of the trees and watched butterflies float and dart around the branches. His mind went to Mandy and re-experienced many of the things that they had shared – the good and the bad. One thing that he was sure of is that he should have been stronger, to support her more so as to support himself. Here she was, this incredible woman, who seemingly had been meant for him and he rejected that support. It was not her, it was him. He could see that he had an inbuilt need to perpetuate his negativity, and by supporting her she would have supported him. But too late now.

∞

After a good night's sleep, he woke up rejuvenated, and so he set off for the day. Feeling fit and strong from the hiking, Stevie felt as if he could run a marathon. It had been a long time since he felt so good. Surveying the landscape, over to the west he saw a large mountain that majestically towered over the rest of the terrain. He had the urge to get to its summit, just for the fun of it. Be good to camp up there, he thought.

It took half a day to get close to the base of the mountain. Most of that time was spent thinking about his time with the Bushmen and the Australian Aboriginals. He considered their community and the love between family members and wondered how different he would be if he had grown up in a loving family.

It was perfect hiking weather as clouds had greyed the sky, keeping it cool. He could only see a part of the mountain as the rest disappeared under cloud. For a short time, he was daunted by the size but quickly put that from his mind.

Studying the best way to go, the terrain started off with a gentle slope that was forest covered but soon became steeper. It was almost vertical when it merged with cloud. The clouds swirled, indicating that it must be windy up there.

With his route in mind he started up the slope and felt the incline steepen as he continued. Within moments his mind wandered. Perhaps he liked hiking because the mind was more malleable than normal. There were times when he took it along a course that he wanted, like the time when he did the Who am I? process. Then there were times when it blanked out and embarked on a pleasant meandering. At other times it expressed its own need and brought to the surface thoughts that must have needed recognition. Sometimes these are of a positive nature and at others, negative and self-defeating. When these happened, with his new skill of awareness he was better able to process these thoughts, and like a curator in a museum, catalogue and place them in their appropriate block for later research. The other thought process was when it drifted over past events in a gentle way. He liked this mind-frame as it was usually gentle, a kind of day dream of the future or past. It was this mind-type that he now had. It was of a fun time of life from about nine to fourteen when he practiced bowling in the cricket nets that were down the road from where he lived. He liked to get away from his foster parents, and so practiced for hours and daydreamed of being a star player.

He enjoyed these times, suspended in daydream glory, hiding reality.

∞

On he strode, through thick bush and under trees. Coming back to the present, he thought about the power of those daydreams and realized how important they were. I didn't become the best cricket player as other goals emerged and changed my focus. Perhaps if I maintained a single focus of the glory, I would have reached the heights that I wanted. Maybe that's what happens to us in life, we let our dreams slide by…

Pausing to catch his breath, he wondered why we do this and so asked his higher-self to give an answer. It instantly returned with numerous insights. The first was that sometimes things just lose their importance. The second answer given was; that we allow them to lose their importance because we fear achieving them or we fear not achieving them. In both cases our subconscious takes over and the dream, well… is sabotaged.

Remembering the conversation with his fear – perhaps they had their way and that is why I was afraid to continue trying to achieve. The answer given by his higher self also told him that his daydream made him a better cricketer at the time, than if not driven by the dream. Daydreams can be good – just don't live in them, and return to be grounded in awareness. He also saw that sometimes it may be pragmatic to let a dream go as there may be things that arrive of greater significance.

Irrespective, awareness of the process was the key. Daydreams can't run on in the background like a distant radio.

He heard a thought from Weishka, "You want to learn more about your intuition?"

"Yeah, sure."

"Good," said Weishka. "You're getting hungry, aren't you?"

"Yep, I am."

"Just in front of you is a ravine that splits into numerous branches and each head towards the top of the mountain. On one of them there is food. When you get to the split you must pause and listen to your intuition to select the correct branch."

It was not long before he saw the ravine, and soon arrived at the split. Stevie paused to focus. Immediately he got the impression that the correct branch was the second last on the right. He was about to take this when his mind interjected, what if it is the one next to it? For a moment he was unsure, but decided to go with the first impression.

It was not long before he came to a bird's nest. It had three eggs in it. The eggs were cold. This suggested to Stevie that the mother had not sat on them for some time. He waited for a while to see if a bird returned but none did. Perhaps she was hurt and can't return? Well, this must be dinner, the eggs would be dead and so with gratitude he will eat them. He was glad he followed the first impression.

∞

Later he was in mist that moved and swirled. One-minute gloom, and another, filtered light. It was alive and active. Soaking wet and almost on his hands and knees, so steep was the incline, he scrambled up. As he got higher he climbed the terrain had changed from floor-forest to rain forest. He was invigorated and so strode on. His breath came in gasps and the temperature dropped as he got higher. His breathing laboured in the thin atmosphere.

Suddenly he broke through the cloud into dazzling sunshine, emerging into yet another terrain of gnarled and stunted trees; he reasoned this was because of the stronger and more persistent wind, plus reduced oxygen in the different climate zone.

Exhausted, he stopped to rest. As he was about to sit on a rock, there it was again – Weishka's stick. Has to be his stick, Stevie thought. He picked it up and tried it for size. It felt good in his hand as he walked. I'll bet he left this for me as support … or some sort of sign. "Thanks, old man!" he shouted.

It was easier walking as there was less bush to work through and he could pick easier routes. Savouring the view until he was on top, he toiled upwards. He could see that the top was not far, perhaps another hour. He was tired from his effort, but good tired, honest tired.

The last ridge was the most difficult as it was a vertical cliff face. The weathered rock offered hand and foot holds. As he finally clambered over the summit, he wondered if all goals were like this, where the last bit always seems to be the hardest?

He was excited he had done the climb and it felt good! He sat to savour the view. Almost as if part of the prize, the wind dropped and the sun had warmed the rocks around him. Clouds hovered around the top, as if to stray too far would leave it unprotected. Far below, the green spread before him until it was absorbed by the horizon.

A large river caught his focus as it weaved across the flat. That's my next destination, he thought, and worked out the way to get there.

He felt that he was not just on top of the world but the only person in it – an empowering feeling. "It's good to set challenges. He saw a parallel in life; that to reach the high peaks where the view is best, you must set the purpose and do the climb."

Towards the west the sun was dropping and cast the silhouette of another mountain. With the fading light he looked to the east one last time before finding a place to sleep for the night. It was getting cold and he was tired.

With a sense of achievement, he fell asleep. There were no dreams, just blissful, nourishing sleep. He told his mind to wake him up before first light so that he could see the sun rise, and so now sat at his view of the world. Far away and well below him there was a smidgen of light that showed the curve of the Earth. Time to go.

Yesterday's upward climb had taken more out of him that he realized. Luckily, being downhill, he did not need as much strength. But his energy levels flagged and he sat to rest.

Weishka's forceful words came to him, "Breath in the life force of the plants around you." This brought his focus back. Well he has been right so many times, he thought. Closing his eyes, he let his intuition take over. It told him to breathe in slowly but deeply, and as he did, he was to imagine seeing light emanating from the plants. He was told to see the light seeping into him. Then with the out breath, push out the tiredness and pass it on to the plants to absorb.

He did this for some time and was pleased at how easily he could focus – he breathed light in, and tiredness out. He had no idea how many breaths he took but suddenly his intuition said "enough".

Opening his eyes, he felt refreshed and calm and was keen to continue towards the river. Not yet, his higher-self told him, thank the plants first …

EMERGENCY ROOM ...
SUNDAY 5:13 PM

Coming on shift Ritchie saw that the patient Jardine was still there. Seeing Rose with the patient, he crossed over to check the instruments and read the chart. There was no change, and the lung inflammation was – just as he thought – critical – the Glasgow Coma Scale now down to a perilous one.

In a firm way, he asked, "Is there anyone who can sign a donor form?"

"Probably the best person to ask is Mandy," said Rose. "She's just about camped here. She is out for a breath of fresh air. She gave me her cell number in case there is any change. Do you want me to give her a call?"

"Yes, do so. If you get her, I'll be about."

∞

Mandy went outside for another break. She thought of the time with Rose, which reminded her of the time after her abortion. She drowned herself in work to deaden the pain, then when at home she retreated to her bed and pulled the covers over her head. She was only starting to recover when the call came to tell her of Stevie's hospitalisation.

And now another call came, this time from Rose. In a daze she move back inside.

∞

Dr Ritchie, pointed Mandy to his office, "Please be seated." Although the office was small it was tidy and organized. "Would you like some coffee?"

Mandy knew they were giving up on Stevie and was numb with grief and tiredness. "No thank you," she sighed.

"He's gone Mandy. There's nothing more we can do for him. Besides, that note he wrote, if he wrote it with a clear mind. He said he does not want to be kept alive with life support". Mandy nodded her understanding.

Richie continued, "We would like permission to conduct brain tests and if all show the same result... ...if only he came in eight hours earlier then perhaps, we could have saved his kidneys from failing, but..."

Mandy just nodded. Her head had dropped, chin to chest – sadness welled up from her throat and cascaded in tears.

Ritchie loved his work but times like these were difficult. He waited for Mandy to compose herself. When she did, he gently said, "Do you know who is the next of kin?"

With a shaky voice she said, "As far as I know there are no living relatives. His foster parents are dead, so there is no one to inform."

"Do you know if anyone has Power of Attorney for him?"

"I do, why?"

"For permission for the brain tests, it's a legal requirement. But also, for another reason..." Ritchie chose his next words carefully, "Stevie's death does not have to be a complete disaster, his organs can be used to save others who can retain a functional life with them. Relatives have the last say if organs can be used, even if a donor registration had been signed by the patient."

Mandy looked at the doctor, and in the same shaky voice said, "He would like that, it was always his way to help others when possible."

"And the tests...?"

Mandy nodded her assent.

Ritchie opened a draw and pulled out a form and pushed it across the desk, "Please will you fill this out..."

∞

"Rose, we have permission for donor use. Here's the form, please organize the paperwork. Keep him on the ventilator so his organs remain alive until pathology comes for him."

"Yes...I'll do so straight away," she said in a quivering voice as she headed off.

The time was 5:27 pm

∞

"Weishka, please tell me more about the dark forces and the fear. Remember when they came to me, they told me that they were my fears and that I have always let them rule me. Could you have stopped them?"

"It would not have served you to have stopped them as you needed to see and understand for yourself. They were right, they have always ruled you. But you learnt the power they had over you, far better than my words could have taught."

"If that is the case, how come I did not recognize their power over me in the past?"

"Remember, on this plane everything is exaggerated or rather on the Earth plane they are muffled by the material density. They were there and showed themselves to you but you chose to ignore them. Here you are forced to see things as they are. The dark forces allow humans to do their work for them. All they have to do is sew negativity… By being fear-based all are kept distant from the light… … Remember the story I told you of Roger, and his soul and ego issues. Well, Roger grew into his understanding but it took most of his life."

EMERGENCY ROOM …
SUNDAY 5:46 PM

With the paperwork completed and authorized, a tear rolled down and off Rose's cheek. She was slumped in the visitor's chair. She did not know how long she sat there as remorse saturated her. She did not know this boy on the bed, but at this stage he was her William, and he was going from her.

Regaining her composure, she got up. Her movements were slow and mechanical. The only sound was an occasional sniff.

Mandy had been outside, on another call of support.

∞

Weishka said to Stevie, "Let's try something. With your current connection, try and slow your mind down even more."

Stevie did and received Weishka's thought form, "Ask a question of the universe and wait for the answer. This can be any question."

He asked about religions and if they serve any value. Instantaneously, a short but succinct understanding came, "If the religious teaching moves one to reverence of all things, then it serves well. If not, it is of little worth."

This is great, Stevie thought, better than Wikipedia, and so asked another question, this time one that was closer to home. "As you know, I have committed suicide or am in the process of dying from doing so. What effect on a soul level will it have?"

Once again, the answer was quick, but was given by way of a question. "What happens to a child who does not do well in a school year and fails?"

Stevie thought, "The child repeats."

"Correct," came the thought form, "you will repeat a life to learn the lessons that you were to learn in this life. There is no purgatory or recrimination as the universe uses self-discipline."

Stevie asked, "And the planet, she has suffered badly. Weishka thinks not... Will she recover?"

"She can if many more people evolve as you have. When there is a critical mass of evolved people all sending love, whilst practicing ecology and the Earth will heal. It is all part of the ascension process."

"What do you mean ascension process?"

"Simply put, it means that the energy consciousness of the entire planet and all people on it will be raised. This is as a result of a massive number of people learning the skills that you have learnt and applying them. You could call it reaching a love quotient."

"So, what does it really mean to be human?" Stevie asked.

"Being human is a method of learning. Your soul knows of the oneness with The Intelligence, but the personality has forgotten and therefore sees itself separate from the intelligence. It lives with the belief of duality. There is nothing wrong with being human and having human experiences. There is nothing wrong with being angry, but get over it quickly. Don't let it rule you. Humans are given the capacity to feel emotions and it is good that they do. It is when the emotions direct the course of life, they sabotage any efforts to understand oneness."

"Living as a human sometimes means being at opposite ends of your soul. For instance, your soul would never mean to embarrass or hurt anyone. Another example is that of a lion. It kills to live but that does not mean its soul would kill, and so to survive it seems at odds with the soul.

Stevie asked, "Then why do we do those things?"

"As a human, you will do these things as that is the learning process, but the sooner you become conscious the better.

Weishka, following the thought questioning process said, "Stop now as you have had enough for one day but remember you can access these thought-form questions any time that you want. All that is required is focus."

EMERGENCY ROOM ...
SUNDAY 7:05 PM

"Calling Nurse Rosemary. Please report to Dr Ritchie. Calling…"

"Yes, Doctor," said a breathless Rose. She had been in the canteen.

"Where the hell is the pathology orderly? We need the instrumentation for another patient who is being brought in by the paramedics. Phone Pathology and get them here in the next fifteen minutes."

"Yes, Doctor, I'll call immediately."

∞

After lighting his fire, it did not take long for Stevie drift into another continent at another period. Weishka let him go on his own. Another journey of learning, this time to America.

Stevie was shocked with the realization that he was in a past life. His name was White Feather, a Tsalagi or as the white people called them, a Cherokee. He was undertaking a ritual to call his power back.

∞

Buffalo strip ripped skin, whilst blood seeped out of wounds that had stretched and festered. With pain tugging at his consciousness, White Feather did not know reality from dream. Still he did not yield to the tiredness.

The blood-stained leather thong was embedded into slits in his skin. The other end attached to the top of the totem pole. This tether was not long enough to allow him to seek the comfort of the ground and so forced him to stand or rotate around the pole in endless circles. There was no respite; if he slumped, the weight of his body stretched the leather and tore the skin. In years to come, his scars would bear testimony to his search for truth.

The different bands of Tsalagi are endowed with different teachings. White Feather's were entrusted with the duty of rekindling the fire of clear mind. The Etowah's had been handed down this responsibility for generations.

The Tsalagi do not use drugs to go into trance. They use fasting, chanting, drumming, and fatigue. The first day, usually with vigour and intent. On the second day exhaustion sets in and the mind starts to float in reality, and into a place where truth is possible.

Time dragged and raced with images enmeshed in delirium and mixed emotions – sad, euphoric, puzzled, regretful, love, hate; all to be worked through to find his happiness.

"Experience is what you get on the way to death, so use it and gain by it. You can't buy it, yet there is a cost as re-learning is expensive. Nor can you swap experience or receive it on a platter".

This seemed to be the theme that came from White Feather's higher self. It spoke of embracing the teaching of experience. Into the future he saw that he was to be a leader and that wisdom was to be within his mind, and so over the days and nights that followed, understanding and clear thinking came.

While Stevie watched, he winced in pain and noticed that his own chest seeped blood.

Deep into the second night, with bitterly cold rain pounding his bent back and bowed head, White Feather remembered a time when as a child, euphoric and feeling warrior-like after shooting a buffalo, he experienced the joy of young speeding legs to the kill. Then abruptly, tears flooded his eyes and rolled down his cheeks as he saw what he had done. His heart exploded in his chest with a grief that has never left him.

He was guided to know sadness, "Feel it," he was told. It was two years before he held a gun again.

The ancestors said, "We are born to undergo experience. Every day is an experience, each minute a time to explore and extend boundaries. Your experiences become your library, always on hand and ready, provided you remember them. All are lessons, pieces in our jigsaw puzzle life. They are processes that must be retained and drawn upon. Sometimes in the process we lose our will. Our strength of mind deserts us and hibernates. White Feather, all your life you have been running away from who you could be. It is time to call back your power – call your happiness back to its place in your heart. If you don't take responsibility for feeling angry and sad, the anger will sit in you and guide you to being less than who you are. Take the time to look deep within. To forgive the past and let go of what might have been, what could have been, and what should have been. Your will is never far away and wants to be reunited with you. Your season of spring is upon you, so call your strength from its hibernation. It is there to serve you but it will only serve you if you consciously call it.

You have surrendered your will and your grief gives you a heavy heart. An excess of grief in people can sadden the Earth. The Earth depends upon us to return the energy, to keep the cycle flowing. If we hold grief to ourselves, we break the flow to Earth. We can return that grief to the Earth by tree-touch, or sit on a rock and tell it your fears. When angry, let the river wash it away. By doing these things we acknowledge our remorse and let the flow continue. When a medicine man heals, he does so by clearing illusion. So, White Feather, let nature be your medicine man, to help with clear thinking."

This was a weird experience for Stevie, witnessing this former life and also feeling the same pain and emotions in this one.

Aching and dizzy, an expansion of the senses, normal colours became iridescent; he was cold in the heat of the day, and hot in the cold night, but the messages continued. Like an ox working a stone mill, round and round the pole plodded his bare feet – shuffling in the dirt, red dust plastered his sweaty frame. Grit caked the corners of his eyes. Later, in retrospect, the hardest part of the initiation was the loneliness. Although always attended by caring elders, he was on his own; no one shared the suffering or filled in the dreary periods when his mind was not visiting the other world.

White Feather knows his ancestors. They have shown themselves to him all his life. His main guide is his grandmother, in life, and afterwards, who taught him good from evil. Then there is Tall Tree, who, true to his name stands tall and straight. It was Tall Tree who taught him patience, telling him that when snow falls on branches and weighs them down, they do not complain. They know that in time it will melt and the sun will shine again. It was Tall Tree and Grandmother who encouraged him to call his happiness.

His ancestors continued – a necessary requirement of experience is for it to come in various forms – the so-called bad experience is a blessing that few understand. It helps to balance, and balance is required for sanity and empathy. The uncomfortable gives body to the comfortable. Experience and emotion are playmates, for emotion is the coating that we wrap around an event to describe it as one to be cherished or regretted.

To White Feather's mind came another event that pained him, a time of arrogance and superiority. How could he take Eonah's girl to play with and discard? Eonah had been his friend. As children they had roamed the hills and valleys, inseparable. Losing Eonah's respect was worse than losing his legs.

White Feather was told by the ancestors that men of knowing make mistakes, but it is men of wisdom that learn from them, and that this bad time and his foolishness would make him stronger, to guide with compassion. And so, we choose our own emotions and therefore select our own worth. One person may see a lesson in an experience, while another may be crushed by it. We are who we are because of our experiences or rather the emotions we attach to them.

White Feather remembered a story from of his youth – a story that burned sadness. The elders call the time the 'Trail of Tears' (a true event). This was in the winters of 1838 and 1839. It was of a forced relocation from their Ancestral Home in present day Oklahoma.

As a child White Feather could not understand how his tribe could tell the story with a forgiving heart. Although the Trail of Tears was generations before White Feather's time, anger rose, like a strong wind. How could the whites be so brutal?

White Feather was told that, "As the white settlers encroached upon our lands, President Andrew Jackson proclaimed his intention to shift us. Our leaders took him to the highest court in the land. We won our case, but Jackson defied the court order and instructed the army to carry out his order.

"We were rounded up like cattle and not allowed to carry possessions. We were forced to walk 800 miles through snow and ice, many had no shoes. We do not know how many of our brothers and sisters perished. Some say 4000, others think it is closer to 8000. They died of exposure, starvation, disease and exhaustion. The white people called it 'Indian removal' – but it was a death march. We were dragged from our spiritual and sacred place of tradition to a land of desolation and so the dark night fell." When the elders spoke of this, it was so vivid that White Feather felt he was there. "The people were not given any warning and were told, 'Go. Go now, with only the clothes on your back. Even much of their food was kept from them."

Yet they spoke about it without bitterness – as if there was no reason for forgiveness. "When you feel the need to forgive, you judge the person from a position of self-given authority. We remember the

Trail of Tears, not from anger or hatred but for the lessons that it has taught us. All humans are good but some do bad things. Even our own have done bad things."

His visions were interrupted by the need to drink water from a supportive elder.

As White Feather got older, his grandmother taught him that, "Not only is there evolution of the body and species but there is spiritual evolution, and that we are moving into a new era. The Trail of Tears episode was wrong, but there was a lesson as it was a lens through which all saw more clearly. It may have been in the past but the effect is still felt. It is a reality for the present, and for the future in as much as the emotion is a tool that reveals anger or allows for forgiveness. The way we think about the Trail of Tears indicates our level of spirituality. The white people started to see the folly of domination of one race upon another. Our dark night helped some on their spiritual way."

The elder's chants continued to the slow beat of the drum, sometimes faltering in a dry throat: (drum) "he hayuya haniwa" (in truth I was conceived) (drum) "he hayuya haniwa" (drum) "he hayuya haniwa", (drum), while bowed legs just supported a body depleted and exhausted.

On the third day, he vomited but there was nothing to bring up, he shuddered violently and gagged. Acid burnt his mouth and the ferocity of it left him weak. So far away was his mind, the sickness and weakness seemed to have happened to someone else.

As a child White Feather's grandmother told him that he would one day take over the teaching of the right mind.

"But how do I do this Grandmother?" he had asked.

"My child, you do it with awareness. It can only be with awareness that you can be with right mind. When in right mind there is no need for forgiveness as you are at one with all. But when not with right mind, anger can take you. White Feather, do you not remember the teachings of Eagle? ... I shall remind you: Eagle is strong and flies to far stars. But Eagle has a weakness. If angry, his wing feathers fall out and he is Earth bound. Only when he buries his anger will he be able to fly again."

His next vision was one where he was taken by his ancestors to a flat area at the top of a rise. The view over the valley was long and wide. A deep vertical hole had been dug. It was an old hole and had been used many times. It was in this hole that White Feather stood, his neck at ground-level. The Ancestors filled the hole with dirt so that only his head remained to be seen. Thus incarcerated, White Feather was immobilized and powerless to remove himself.

Stevie shuddered as if he was in the hole.

The ancestors told White Feather, "This is how you see your life, powerless to do anything. It is now time to call back your power. By doing so you will live. By not doing so you will perish. White Feather we leave you with one tool. The tool is the most important tool you have been given. You have always had this tool. Like all tools it can be put to useful service, but used incorrectly it can damage you. That tool White Feather is your mind." And then they were gone.

White Feather panicked at the thought of this slow death. "This is not learning… this is torture."

Stevie knew this horror and was familiar with the panic and fear. He drew parallels between his life as Stevie and that of White Feather.

It was for good reason that the Ancestors had White Feather faced the valley. To start with he did not see the view, so consumed with the fear his mind fed him.

It was not long before an ant found him, drawn by the smell of meat. It climbed up White Feather's left cheek and took a bite to assess the value of its find. Exploring further, it entered the moist cavity of a nostril, where it paused and drank before going higher up the passage.

White Feather felt the ant with its first footstep on his face. He tried to shake his head to dislodge it but there was not enough movement. The bite released a fresh avalanche of fear. He had two points of awareness, the one that death was going to be long and painful. The other was that he felt every footfall of the ant as it scaled his cheek and entered his nose.

The ant expressed pheromones that other ants could smell, and so it was not long before other ants came, first, in ones and twos, then by the dozens.

White Feather wondered if he would go crazy before he died. By now his face was swollen from the toxins that the ants injected. He squeezed his eyelids together to try and keep them from entering his eye-sockets. The ants were in his ears and mouth, and everywhere they went they bit and tasted. It seemed that there were fifty marching in an out of his nostrils. Some seemed to go up as far as his brain. He cried in anguished self-pity and pain. "This is no way for a human to die. I have been forsaken by my own people."

He opened his eyes as if to gain inspiration. Once his eyes adjusted to the harsh sunlight, he saw the home of his upbringing. He saw the animals and nature that had surrounded his childhood...

As he took this in, an eagle flew into his view. He watched and longed for its freedom. The lesson of the eagle as told by his mother and grandmother came to him. For the first time the strength of the story claimed a ledge in his mind to strengthen and grow. For the first time he understood how weak of mind he had become. He saw that its affect was slow forming, like mould on a wet rock.

Somehow, seeing the eagle and remembering the story brought clarity. "No more," he shouted. He looked at the eagle and shouted, "I see you... I may die here, but I will die with character and clear mind."

He forced to his mind gratitude. If he was going to die, he would do it with gratitude. He brought many remembrances to his mind. Each was examined and turned around and looked at from all angles. He released the anger from the Trail of Tears and other anguishes. Although the ants were still there, he had less awareness of them.

Not only did he look at the happy memories, he looked with gratitude at the sad events of his life for what they taught him. He sent love to his friend Eonah, and was grateful to have learnt the lesson of self-forgiveness.

Hours passed as he examined the hurts and sadness of his life. He gave love to all of them and took responsibility. He was purged and prepared for death. Death I am ready with clear mind.

Without realizing it, White Feather had claimed his power. And as he did there was a surge of power. The Ancestors smiled and were pleased.

They knew that White Feather had called his power, called his happiness. They reminded him that it was the Eagle who came to help him. They went on to tell him that it was known that Eagle was his totem animal and it is for that reason he was given the name White Feather and that Eagle's wing feathers are white. Like Eagle, you lost your tail feathers when you became angry, and like Eagle you were grounded. Now that you have called back your will you can fly to far stars.

∞

White Feather knew that the initiation was over when the dreams and visions ceased and the awareness of his surroundings returned. The lessons ended as quickly as a summer storm leaves, its power spent.

Although weary, White Feather was grateful for the time shared with his ancestors. Concerned elders supported his tortured body, and gently cut the thongs. He was supported to a specially constructed shelter to rest and reflect.

It took him weeks to recover physically, but what he learnt remained with him for the rest of his days. There would come a time when he would take his place amongst his people, to guide and lead.

∞

Stevie knew that he had been White Feather in that life. He could see how in that life he had lost his way, as he had done in his current life. As White Feather had called back his power, I, Stevie, will call back mine. There was a surge of hope and courage coursing through his body.

∞

Aware of the passing time, and unaware of Earth time, Stevie went back to the hospital ward.

He saw the plump nurse slumped in a chair. She appeared to be crying. He could see the paperwork saying he is to be taken to the morgue.

Panicked, he knew he had to make his decision, to go down the tunnel of light, or return. A part of him wanted to go back and take on the challenges of life. There was another part of him that screamed, "No!"

Not being able to locate the source of this fear he could not bargain or reason with it. He knew he had cleared many of the issues that bound him but there still must be something… what… what is it? he wondered.

Returning from the hospital to continue his hike to the river, he picked up Weishka's stick. At first, he rushed and consumed the ground with great strides, but bringing himself to balance slowed down. It was a hot day, probably the hottest on the journey. Ahead the sky was blue but he could see a storm building, a far dark band on the horizon.

He took his shirt off and wrapped it around his waist. Brown from the sun and lean from the exercise he strode down the slope. As the storm came closer, the light became surreal. He could feel the power within the approaching storm that was about to be unleashed. Although only three in the afternoon the indigo curtain that descended made it appear like night. Partnering the lightning and thunder, wind hummed through the trees. Branches broke into a wild dance, stripping leaves and tore at grass. And then the rain came. At first tentative, and then with full force. It came as if it had never rained before, so hard the drops bounced knee height up off the ground.

Stevie had been walking for about two hours and was invigorated. Excited by the energy of the storm he continued. With Weishka's stick held lightly and horizontal to the ground in his right hand. It gave balance to a rhythm of swinging arms and moving legs. The rough stick felt good in hand and as the stick arched forward, his left arm synchronized backwards. His breath was deep but smooth and helped to bring mind and body together. The rhythmic movement gave an expansion of mind, and at that moment he knew he did not need to make any decisions that the answer would come in its own time.

Coupled to the energy of the storm he felt invincible, the very essence of nature. Little did he know that this would be the last time that he would have freedom of movement.

As his body parts were one in a dance, so was his mind – all was one. There was no difference between himself and the forest – the rain, lightning, the puddles underfoot, and his glistening torso with rivulets of rain running down his body.

The storm, wanting to purge as much territory as possible moved on, allowing the stunned land to recover. Ruffled birds returned and sang back the sun. The late afternoon light was soft and gentle, caressing the bruised terrain. Elongated shadows gave a gentleness that was at odds with the powerful storm.

With the softening light, the *adrenaline* diminished from Stevie's system. But still the connection to all remained. Sitting on a rocky overhang he asked his higher-self to show him the blockage – why he was scared to return to his body. Almost immediately a baby came to him. It was small, doll-like. The eyes round and blue, the skin fair. It telepathically said, "Steven, in this life of mine, you fathered me. I have much to be grateful for. You gave me life, which gave me teaching. As development of my soul, I needed the experience you gave me. Look deeper behind your eyes and you will see what causes your blockage."

Stevie did, and was taken back to the time when he received a letter from Mandy. It was a short message… *I have just aborted our child… …I could not allow it to come into a home of sadness. I have always loved you but you have been so irresponsible... As I could not reach you, it became my responsibility. I cannot tell you how bad I feel, all I want to do is to curl up and go to sleep – forever. I am so sad…*

Stevie saw himself shriek out as if stabbed in the heart, "I have killed my child."

His vision changed to Mandy and he saw her in a café. He could not see who she was talking to but saw and heard her say, "I killed them both." He saw her break down.

Interrupting his thoughts, he heard the voice of his child say, "You think you killed me. Mandy thinks she killed me. The truth is that I chose both of you as the vehicle of my experience. On a universal level, no one loses. I have had the experience. Mandy has her own growth reason, which I am not permitted to share with you. And you,…you… you have tried to kill yourself… partly because you could not cope with the agony of my death, a death you felt you contributed to. We were all in this together, and all is perfect. For you Stevie, my biological father, it is not easy to become a master, as the worst pains and emotions have to be overcome. You are almost there but this last boundary is to be surmounted."

Stevie asked in a voice that was barely audible, "What is that boundary?"

As soon as he heard the answer, he knew he was free. The answer was, "Forgive yourself!"

∞

"We both know what you are going to do, don't we?" said Weishka. "I have known for some time of your intention to reclaim your body and your life. But first you have some concerns that you would like me to address, don't you?"

"Please, can we hurry?" asked Stevie, with concern.

Weishka chuckled whilst hearing Stevie's first question, "Will you be there for me, can I call on you?"

"If it is not me, it will be some other form of help. You will not be abandoned – you are never abandoned. And remember you have your higher-conscious to call on."

"Will I retain awareness?"

"Yes, if you have the desire and put your mind to it."

"I'm worried that once I am back in the same routine and job I will lapse back into the old state of negativity."

"As long as you remember who you are at all times you will be fine. You have learnt much and it is important that you keep this at the forefront of your mind…Try and keep in mind that your physical vibration must always be in line with your soul vibration.

Stevie, I want you to think about your question of lapsing back into the same old routine. You don't have to do this, you know that. Remember it is not the job that is the problem, it is the attitude that you bring to the job. There is honour in all work. With awareness you can know that honour, and when you do, let it live and it will grow and manifest a new vocation…

"With your new awareness you will only attract positive and happy events to your life. Your old friends that latched onto you and sucked the goodness out of you in a dance of mutual weakness will fall off and slip unnoticed from your life. They will be replaced by people of greater spiritual awareness. Remember, like vibrations attract like vibrations."

Stevie thought, "I'm excited and scared at the same time."

"Stevie there is no need to be scared when you trust. Fear is separation of trust. By keeping the awareness, you remain balanced."

"Please explain balance again, but hurry, there is not much time."

"To balance requires the awareness to tell you that you are momentarily lost and far from connection. That is the first step. Step two is acknowledging being disconnected. The third is to consciously relax and focus on reconnecting. Whilst doing this you allow your worries and fears to drop off you. When in a calmer state you bring to mind reverence of all. This will allow you to remember to trust."

Counting his fingers, Weishka continued, "This, I believe has four steps, but it all starts with awareness. And the more you do these four steps, the faster you go from helplessness to equanimity or as I prefer to call it – balance."

In an excited voice, Stevie said, "I got it."

Weishka continued, "One of the things that pushes people out of balance is other people. There are people in your world that are out of balance, as you were. There are criminals, and crooked politicians. Mankind, can be a jungle with much savagery, there is greed, poverty and selfishness. Humans get lost in all of this, and react from a place of fear. Hate and resentment kicks in, as does, excessive sadness. You must always keep balanced, be aware. Let those people have their own journey, and do not let the gross negativity affect you. Your job is balance, trust that you will be 'looked after', always reach towards the light, even in the storm of humanity."

Stevie was quiet for a while thinking about his next question. Weishka interrupted with, "Your next question – how will you help mankind with your newfound knowledge. Can I go ahead and explain?" Stevie nodded.

"Well the first thing to understand is that you are not an evangelist…"

"Thank God for that," interrupted Stevie.

"Nor do you need to stand on a soap box and try to convince anyone to repent. You don't have to tell them that if they don't listen to you that they are for the flames of hell. All *you* do is be connected. Be aware and that if what you 'are' appears good, you will attract only those who are ready to learn. Your light will spread far and wide, seen by those who are ready to see it. Your being will be like perfume – you may put it on yourself, but many will get its essence. Stevie, you must understand that when you go back you will be like a living master."

Stevie gulped, "No way, I can't be a master. I am weak and get angry. I have been so selfish."

"No, you don't have to be, not when you are aware and balanced. You claim your spirituality in the moment. Just remember who you are."

"Now that I understand The Intelligence better, how best do I connect to it… I mean Christians pray to what they call God, and Islamic people bow to the east several times a day. For me to know it better what do I do or say to It".

Weishka replied with, "You can pray or prostrate yourself if you wish, but that is a bit like talking of your connection. Whereas, awareness and showing the feeling of love and gratitude is a stronger connection. Only in doing this does the connection get strong. To know it, you have to feel it, and it is the feeling that is the important part. Only when you plunge into its depths will it quietly reveal itself".

"Weishka, you're talking code again. Can you explain it in a more simplistic way. But hurry."

"No. There is no simplistic way to describe the Infinite, but listen to the words … plunge and feel.

"I have learnt much on this etheric journey and want to help people to a better life. How can I teach the same back there where everything is so much denser?"

"Remember, at the start of the journey, you asked where your supplies will come from? At the time I did not say that this is a benevolent universe, but it is, it will work out okay."

Stevie was excited, but was aware that Weishka seemed to carry concern in his usually happy face. "Okay, what's wrong?"

"It's best that I show you. Come."

Stevie found himself back at the hospital. Weishka said, "Scan your energy field."

Stevie knew something was desperately wrong and said, "Is… is it too late… for me to return?"

"No, you can return. Scan your body."

It did not take Stevie long to see his energy field. It was thick and flat and only emanated three centimetres from his body. The colour was an insipid yellow, which he intuited as being weak. At first, he did not see the spots, but as he watched they became prominent. There were three, two where he thought his kidneys would be. One was much larger than the other. The third blob was on the side of the brain.

Not understanding, he asked, "What do they mean?"

"They mean that you have damaged your body. As you intuited, the two lower blobs are your kidneys. One has completely failed, and the other has lost much capacity."

Fearing the worst, Stevie asked, "And the one on the side of the brain?"

"You are likely to have mobility problems. Look at your left arm, I think you missed that."

Stevie did, and for the first time saw a grey shadow down his left arm. He was quiet as he thought of the implication of returning to a damaged body and ill health.

Weishka waited for Stevie's decision. It was not long coming.

"White Feather called his power, I will call mine, there still can be happiness… and growth… and the value of service to others. And now, as Steven Jardine, even with these disabilities, I'll call my happiness and will. I will negotiate with my circumstances and get on as best as possible. Every day I will fight for survival, I will keep my connection. I have learnt well, I will live those lessons. I will still be the subtle voice that will offer compassion, wisdom, gentleness, and of course love. Weishka I am grateful for your love and support… But I still think that you dress funny. Oh, and here is your stick back. Thank you for it as it helped me get up the mountain.

"I do have one last question for you. Why did you come to help me? The reason why I ask this is that millions of people need the support of a helper, an angel, such as yourself. Yet I was lucky enough to get that help, where most don't."

"My friend, you do not need to thank me as I am a gift from the universe. Much the same as you are a gift from the universe. Even though you did not know it, you were ready to listen and allowed your soul to show you the way. In your case you listened, many don't. They will when they are ready. Your soul was living with the integrity of its task, that is, to claim your aspect of the Intelligence.

When open to it, the universe will shower you with infinite opportunities. Many will go by unnoticed, many will seem too difficult to obtain. This is unfortunate as no opportunity is given that you can't handle. And many are just not acted upon. But this is fine as you all have freewill. We won't do it for you, but know that your abundance is all around you, all you have to do it to pick it up and make it yours – just as you learnt.

This is not farewell, there is never farewell. In this life of yours, I had the privilege of showing you. In the next, you may show me.

And so, in the land of the Kalahari, where I once lived as a Bushman, I say, stand in your power, and be the best you can, even with deformities."

∞

The cord seemed to retract and Stevie felt himself being pulled backwards at rapid speed towards his body. There was a time of horizontal hovering just above the body, when suddenly, sucked into it, he re-joined it. As the two bodies merged there was a distinct slapping sound as if to snap the two together.

EMERGENCY ROOM ...
SUNDAY 7:29 PM

"Took you long enough," Rose said to the orderly. "Another patient needs it."

"Sorry but we had an emergency," said the tall but soft-spoken orderly. "Okay, please sign the form that we removed... what's his name... oh yes, Steven Jardine... and the time is? ... Who are you?" he asked as Mandy wandered in.

Answering for Mandy, Rose said, "The patient's partner."

"Please get her out, not good for her to see this."

Rose crossed to Mandy, "Come, let me help you." As she said this, she motioned that Mandy must turn around and go out with her.

Sensing what was happening, Mandy collapsed in the visitors' chair. Rose bent to place a comforting hand on Mandy's head and said, "Come now dear, there is no point in staying here."

Unable to compose herself, Mandy sobbed, her body shuddered in great racking waves. Respecting the situation, the orderly waited and hoped that the young lady would soon be fine. As he did, his eyes fell onto the monitor. "What the hell?! This guy's not dead. There's movement on the monitor."

Rose was up in flash. At first, she thought he was mistaken. Instead of the flat line, there was a slight quiver. For a full twelve seconds she stared without comprehension. Coming to her senses she shouted, "James! James!" as she rushed to the other side of the ward to where Ritchie was taking the pulse of an elderly gentleman. "James! Come quickly, you won't believe it."

Mandy stood up, "What is it? What does this mean...?"

Ritchie was not aware of the use of his first name by his head nurse as he was caught in her excitement. Arriving at the bedside he glanced at the monitor. "What... a slight pulse?... blood pressure rising, as is oxygen uptake"

With professional speed his stethoscope found its place in his ears. The other end went straight to Stevie's chest, whilst his other hand took Stevie by the wrist to feel for a pulse. "Quickly, do a Glasgow Coma Rating", he said to Rose.

Ritchie shone his torch into Stevie's eyes and saw pupil dilation. He could not believe what he was seeing and returned his gaze to the monitor. Gradually, the line gained animation. Within a few minutes, Rose announced, "The rating is now seven".

"His pulse is strengthening," Rose whispered.

"What does this mean? Is he recovering?" asked Mandy

Shaking his head in disbelief, Ritchie looked at Rose and shrugged his shoulders. "Mandy… he is brain dead, and even if he survives, he is likely to have brain damage… He'll also have renal failure."

All were quiet, but quiet turned to a hum of excitement as they watched the line showing the pulse and blood pressure increase.

All four literally held their breath for fifteen minutes as the alternatively looked at Stevie, or the monitors. It seemed an eternity.

Stevie eyes slowly flutter. Other than the instruments, all were quiet. Finally, his eyes opened. For more minutes Stevie stared unblinking and without focus, a glazed look. But, like the adjusting of a camera, clarity came, and the eyes started to blink and gain focus. Everything seemed heavy. Gone was the lightness of his etheric body. His eyes, wandered around the bed area.

Looking over him, he saw the happy face of a middle-aged nurse. He felt her squeeze his hand and returned the smile.

Stevie had seen the interaction between Mandy and Ritchie, and heard the comment, "... even if he survives, he is likely to have brain damage… He'll also have renal failure." When he heard this, he smiled to himself, for he knew the power of the mind and belief, and what is possible of our incredible brain. Weishka also chuckled at this limiting belief.

Behind the smiling nurse he saw a small African man, bent almost double and leaning on a crooked stick. The man raised an arm, "Tshjamm." Stevie winked at the African.

They all wondered to whom the wink was aimed as there was no one in that direction. Richie thought that his prognosis of Stevie being mentally impaired was correct.

Stevie's eyes fell on Mandy. He tried to reach his left arm out to her. It had no life.

He could see that she had lost weight. Her cheeks were hollow and her face red and blotchy from her recent crying. Seeing that he saw her, a nervous smile formed on her lips as she waited to his response of her being there.

She did not have to wait long before he said in a dry and cracked voice, "I am going to hold you to your promise."

Perplexed, she asked, "Promise… What promise?"

Feeling a joy that he did not know possible he replied, "The promise that you made to the angels. Do you remember?"

For a second, she did not understand but then it dawned on her as she remembered her silent prayer. The attempted smile grew wide and strong. "How did you know of the promise?" she asked.

"Oh, the Angels told me."

THE END

A F T E R W O R D

Three years later; the following is an excerpt of an interview with Steven Jardine of the 'Happiness Foundation' published in a leading magazine.

Interviewer's question, "And now, with the teachings that you offer, how has it affected you?"

Answer

Where there was turmoil, there is now calm

Where there was frustration, cohesion resides

Where there was financial ruin, there is abundance

Where there was a sickly body, health, strength and energy are now to be had

Where there was anger, there is peace

Where there was self-condemnation, confidence resides

Where there was separation, there is trust

Where there was selfishness, compassion fills me

Where there were demons, all are gone

Where there was grumpiness, happiness flows

Where once there was demanding, there is now only gratitude

And, where there was nothing but misfortune, there is luck

Where fear filled every fibre of my body, there is no more fear, only hope and optimism

Where I was once alone, I now see the support of many unseen hands, all guiding and loving

Where there was illusion, there is clarity and understanding

Where all was difficult, now all is easy

When once I had to win at all costs, I can now let go and just be

Where my life was a siege with blockages, all flows

Where there was nothing, there is nothing but love

Question; And how did these changes happen?

Answer; Because I called my power and happiness. By doing so I moved to the light, understanding and love.

Question; can I also do this?

Answer; Of course, you can. All can, but it takes mindfulness and a willingness to trust. I have learnt of the importance of slowing down and listening to the silent voice within…"

∞

This manifesto of the Happiness Foundation has a curious logo, it was of a seagull with a deformed leg.

∞

And the nurse, Rose, was one of the first to benefit from Stevie's teachings. You may remember that she blamed herself for the death of her son William. Stevie taught Rose that William was responsible for his own actions. She also learnt about love for herself, which became a way of life for her. And although she misses William, she is able to have a functional and happy life. She also has become the godmother to Stevie and Mandy's two-year-old baby boy, Lance, who has the nickname 'Weishka'.

∞

Lessons as taught by the Happiness Foundation:

Four Steps as outlined by Weishka to return to balance:

1) to balance requires the awareness to remind you when you are momentarily lost.

2) acknowledging being disconnected

3) to consciously relax and focus on reconnecting. Whilst doing this you allow your worries and fears to fall off you.

4) when in a calmer state you bring to mind the greatness of all. This will allow you to remember to trust.

Weishka said, "And the more you do these four steps, the faster you go from helplessness to equanimity or as I prefer to call it, balance."

Discussion points as taught by the Happiness Foundation: (concepts, Stevie learnt in the story). **It includes a place for your own notes.**

Perhaps make copies of these so you can fill it in numerous times.

If you knew of the alternative way of being, your life could be a happy life.

What are these?

____

____

____

____

____

____

____

Modern mankind is in this dire situation it is because humanity has lost their connection to the sacred. *How are you gaining your connection?*

____

____

____

____

____

By calling our power, we as a clan continue.

If you are not happy, it is your fault — why?

____

____

____

____

____

Unless, and until man embarks on this quest of the true self, doubt and uncertainty will follow his footsteps through life.

What is your true self?

____

____

____

____

____

If you align yourself with that power, then not only will your life have a purpose, it will work better.

Give examples of how you will align yourself.

____

____

____

____

____

By sacrificing this life before you master those lessons, then in your next incarnation, you will be confronted with the same lessons.

What are your lessons?

____

____

____

____

____

I want you to address all animals, plant life and microscopic life with reverence, and when you do it will change you.

Have you started to do this, and with what results?

____

____

____

____

The soul within a body has greater power than the ego.

Your thoughts on ego, and your ego?

There is intelligence in animal migration, cell division and biology, as there is in all nature. This is the Intelligence that I refer to. This Intelligence is the creative and organizing power behind all forms of life.

How have you experienced this?

To go back no wiser than when you came, your life is likely to be much the same as it was. *Record your growth.*

When you understand love, you can't help but be grateful.

Are you encouraging your heart to smile?

Gratitude is an aspect of love (love for yourself)

Write down your efforts to feel gratitude for today.

If religion does not lead you to reverence of all things, then it is of little worth.

Do you agree? And why?

Referring to: visualizing, manifesting, creating abundance and all sorts of other terms; The concept is a good one but does not normally work. The reason is that most people do not trust that it can happen. They are locked in the mind set of dualities where The Intelligence or God is different to them. By believing in this separateness, how can they manifest? They can't is the answer.

What sort of life do you want to manifest?

____

____

____

____

Could it be that Love and the Intelligence are the same thing?

If so, how does this make you feel and act?

____

____

____

____

We are your fears Stevie, we rule you.

What fears rule you?

After a time, his mind and body fused into one, and the noise of silence diminished.

Give experiences of your meditations – your quiet times?

It is in silence that you reach beyond yourself.

What has your Higher Self shown you about yourself?

You create for tomorrow what you are today. And so, if you are without fear now, the next day will be better.

By now you should have experienced this. Give examples.

Humanity's situation is also the result of their combined thoughts. Energy does not direct itself; it is propelled to create from the direction given. It does not care. It is like a genie from a bottle that will grant you any wish, irrespective of it being good for you or not. So, for the things you want in life you must propel the energy in the right way.

Give examples.

This moment is just one frame of all moments that make up all time.

Explain this concept.

That our mind can be a traitor that robbed happiness and optimism.

Give examples from your life.

____

____

____

____

____

You, and all humans create your own reality, whether you do this intentionally or not. But here is the important point; by creating your own reality you manipulate or develop the illusion of this material plane. Conversely, the illusion you live in, is a reflection of what you have created.

Explain to yourself your illusions and how they have ruled your life in the past.

____

____

____

____

When in awareness you become Wisdom observing itself, and that is why it felt so good – *Did you find this to be true to yourself?*

...it is your journey; the teachings will find you.

What lessons have been given to you in the past that you have ignored?

A firm commitment must be made to reclaim your power, your will, your happiness.

If you are now doing this, *explain the results. If you are not doing it, why?*

Go through each (past) feeling but this time don't feel inadequate – feel a surge of power, claim you power and let it swamp inadequacy.

Write these down.

He now knew he was nature, not external to it.

Do you agree? Why?

Stevie wondered if all goals were like this, where the last bit always seems to be the hardest.

Do you agree?

Living as a human sometimes means being at the opposite of your soul. For instance, your soul would never mean to embarrass or hurt anyone. A lion kills to eat but its soul would not kill if it had a choice.

Where have you been at the opposites with your soul?

____

____

____

____

____

White Feather knew he had surrendered his power... His grief and resentment made his heart heavy. *An excess of grief in people can sadden the Earth.* The Earth depends upon us to return the energy, to keep the cycle flowing. If we hold grief to ourselves, we break the flow to Earth. You can return that grief to the Earth by tree-touch, or sit on a rock and tell it your fears. When angry, let the river wash it away. By doing these things you acknowledge your remorse and let the flow continue. When medicine man heals, he does so by clearing illusion, so let nature be your medicine man, to help to clear thinking.

Your thoughts on this?

____

____

A bad experience is a blessing that few understand. It helps to balance, and balance is required for sanity and empathy. The uncomfortable gives body to the comfortable. Experience and emotion are playmates, for emotion is the coating that we wrap around an event to describe it as one to be cherished or regretted.

What blessings have you had, or could have from (seemingly) bad experiences.

The way we think about the Trail of Tears indicates our level of spirituality. Many started to see the folly of domination of one race upon that of another. Our dark night helped some on their spiritual way.

How have you embraced this philosophy?

Spirituality is actively living these beliefs. Each time you ask, "Who am I?" you further your knowledge. You become open to more questions and answers, and as you learn more, more questions arrive.

So, who are you?

Another name for personality is collective experience.

Using the last question (above) as a guideline, why have your collective experiences made you who you seem to be?

And what can you do about it?

No, there is no simplistic way to describe The Infinite, but listen to the words … it is only when you plunge into its depths that is quietly reveals itself.

Have you plunged?

It's like when you are asleep, you are asleep. But when you wake up, you can wake up more. The way you had the awareness when sitting under the tree is the way you must be when in your body.

Are you really awake when you think you are awake?

Remember it is not the job that is the problem, it is the attitude that you bring to the job. There is honour in all work.

What is your attitude towards your job and the company you work for?

____

____

____

____

____

Respect is a subtle aspect of love and so the respect that they showed to the terrain, the animals, the bush and trees as well as all humans was of love.

What respect (and compassion) do you have for all life forms?

____

____

____

____

____

They are locked in a mind-set of duality where The Intelligence is different to them. By believing in separateness, how can they manifest? They can't is the answer.

Do you recognise that your happiness lies in your connection and understanding of The Intelligence?

Your old friends latched onto you and sucked the goodness out of you in a dance of mutual weakness. They will fall off, and slip unnoticed from your life. They will be replaced by people of greater spiritual awareness. Remember, like vibrations attract like vibrations.

Have you found this to be true?

Even though you did not know it, you were ready to listen and allowed your soul to show you the way.

Do you believe this? Explain why.

____

____

____

____

____

…but there is no such thing as fate. Fate is a copout used by humans to avoid responsibility. These people say that it is divinely orchestrated. I can tell you that you exert control over your own life through acknowledging the process, and the sending of love. Fate only occurs if you believe it to be so.

Explain this in greater detail.

____

____

____

____

… there is no such thing as bad karma. Look at karma as a lesson to overcome. (Remember that karma can also be good karma)

Explain how being positive and compassionate will smooth out life's impediments.

I did not give you the value of life, you had it already. You just needed to take it out of the wardrobe and put it on.

Where do you find value in life — in living?

Westerners may have known the sciences, but they did not know about spiritual law. And for me, I know which is the most important. This view reflects who was really advanced and who ignorant (refer below for this wisdom).

Explain how these spiritual laws can uplift your life.

… he carried the awareness of Weishka's suggestion, of holding all that he came in contact with, with reverence. He had noticed that there was a subtle change to the way he perceived things. At first, he could not put his figure on it but there was definitely something to it. After a time, he realised that by showing reverence he was making a connection across consciousness. Weishka has been saying all along that everything is of consciousness, that all is connected, and that all you have to do is look for it, and the connection will become obvious. He was seeing and feeling what he had always been connected to but did not recognise the connection.

What does the above mean to you?

In this life of yours, I had the privilege of showing you. In the next, you may show me.

Do you believe that if who you are is good, that it will help others? If so, explain why this is so.

Service to others is a way to happiness.

Are you willing to try service and see its results? If so, write down how you would like to start.

The story of Roger showed; From Fear To Love is a Spiritual Journey offering the choices that he made throughout his life to become the person who he could be. Offering understanding about the fear that blocks his path to inner peace and denies him his love. It opens a spiritual path, encouraging him to follow a journey that gives freedom from the tyranny of fear so that he can grow."

You must keep practicing this, and you will find that you will be more in love than fear.

Write down you result as you practice sending love to yourself.

He had listened and heard his intuition. He wished he had that knowledge when it woke him up that time when it sat on him. He knew a life long fear now had no control over him. He also realised that this was the first time in his life that he has actually stopped to face any fear that he may have had. He had always run, lashed out, got drunk to mask it – anything but face it.

What fears has this story helped you understand?

____

____

____

____

____.

Do you run and lash out?

____

____

____

____

____

EXTRA NOTES

T H E
D E V E L O P M E N T
O F   T H E   S T O R Y

There can never be one starting point for the germination of a book. It is possible that the book formed in my mind many years ago. But this is not the point that I want to discuss now. It is the entity or helper in the story called Weishka, who is the subject of this section.

His first appearance in my life came some ten years before the concept of the story grew within my conscious mind. That does not mean to say that the reason for the work was not formed in another dimension or energetic form.

I first saw Weishka when reversing out of my driveway one dusk. He was just as I described in the story, that is; little, in fact tiny, and almost bent doubled. The crooked stick supported his horizontal back. Of course, after my double-take, he was gone. Clearly, he was an entity from another plane.

For many evenings after that I looked for him, hoping for his return as I was convinced, he had shown himself to me for a reason. But there was no sign of him.

For a moment I shall digress, as months before that encounter with Weishka I had a compelling drive to write this book. However, I had no idea of what I was to write.

The next event in this curious episode was when I was having a clairvoyant reading from a medium. It was towards the end of the session, when I asked the channeller, "Who was the entity that I saw when driving out of my drive?" I said nothing more about the entity, his race or appearance.

The reply was, "Oh that would be an African, of the Bushman race, I think."

After I nodded yes, I asked, "So why did he come to me?"

"You will be working with him some time in the future."

"Doing what?"

"I don't know, I can't get that or when it will be."

So that was it, but over the months he remained real and somehow present to me.

Two years later, this unknown story agitated, determined to be told, and so I wrote to see what may emerge. What I had written did not fit the story that was to later emerge. As a writer, I had learnt to listen to the little voice that nags, especially when it shouted, "It's not right, write it again." And so, I did, and this time included more of Stevie's attempted suicide. When my pen started to describe the leaving of Stevie's body, that's when Weishka, the entity, came to me as a vivid picture in my mind. He directed the course of the next phase of writing and the dialogue between him and Stevie.

I wondered, could it be possible that my African, whose name I did not know at that stage, was really a part of the story. It was not long before I was to get confirmation, in fact, only a week. It was when having a chat and tea with friends, Linda and Peter, when Linda stopped in mid-sentence, as she received a message. She said, "I have just been interupted by my guides; they say that you are working with Serapis Bey."

"Who's that?" I asked.

"An ascended master," was her reply, "have you not heard of him?"

I hadn't, but my thoughts were thrown into turmoil when she interrupted with, "I seem to remember that Serapis Bey had an incarnation as a Bushman. I nearly dropped my tea cup."

Later, when reading about Serapis Bey, the writer claimed that when, as the incarnation of a Bushman that it was of the early Bushman, many hundreds of years ago.

The next confirmation was a few days later. This was as a result of asking for synchronicities on the matter. Let me explain. Whenever I need confirmation on something that I am working on, I ask The Intelligence for several confirmations as several eliminates the possibility of coincidence – boy did I get synchronicities.

At that time, I would normally get about sixty emails a day, and so over the thirty thousand emails that I had received up to then, I don't ever recall receiving any on the Bushman race. The next day after my request to the universe, I received two emails, both from different senders, both within an hour of each other, and both with completely different content. In other words, it was not the same email as if sent as a group sending. In the contents of both there were photos of Bushmen, of course different photos of different Bushmen in different areas. Weishka looked like these Bushmen, only he was dressed in Western clothes.

Then, the next confirmation came about a month later when visiting a friend, Lee, she asked, "Have you read this?" she said, whilst handing me the book, *The Lost World of the Kalahari*, by Laurens Van der Post. This book, which was published in 1958 was about the Bushman, and Van der Post's was the first work to document these almost extinct people of Africa. At that stage, my friend Lee did not know about my book or the Bushman connection.

The pictures in the email and the book showed a people who have a similar size and facial features as the entity I saw in my driveway. Certainly, Weishka was of Bushman heritage.

Then as I was writing the book, it soon became clear that Weishka was not just channelling lessons for Stevie, he was also channelling them for me. Much that he taught Stevie I already knew but much I didn't.

Now that the book is finished, it will be interesting to see if Weishka continues to work with me. I hope that he does but time will tell.

NOTES

Australian Aborigines, Native Americans, and Kalahari Bushmen of Africa

What I am about to relate are my thoughts pertaining to these three cultures offered before being colonised by Europeans.

All three offered gratitude for all in life. All read the land, they have a relationship and contact with spirits (ancestors). They believed in reincarnation. Telepathy was a commonly used ability. There is a connection and symbiotic relationship with plants, trees, rocks, water and all animal types. They used only for their immediate needs and regarded themselves as caretakers for the following generations. This ethos of looking after the Earth as caretakers, is borne out by the fact that they are the oldest continuous races in the world, and until Western man came, they retained enough resources for sustainability. They never owned the land or anything upon it. How could they, as life maintained itself through partnership. Sacred respect for life and nature is at the forefront of thought. All animals, plants and life forms are thanked for their sacrifice. Nomadic, not because they liked to travel, but because they did not want to deplete an area of its resources. An abhorrence of exploitation of any kind so sharing what little they had was never debated. Love for fellow man and all forms of life. They understand the oneness, and that all is dependent and interdependent on each other. Nature and humans are all part of the same breath. They were aware that when they ate of plants, roots, and animals that its life force was commuted into the body of the eater. All three-practice ritual and passage of right that incorporates nature and spiritual awareness. Although they worshipped different gods, all ultimately blended into one, and all the gods were seen as benevolent. Respect for God was given in partnership, where respect was returned in kind. The relationship with ancestors or spirits was one of learning where teaching was handed down.

Respect is a subtle aspect of love and so the respect that they showed towards the terrain, the animals, the bush and trees as well as all humans was of love.

Reading the land was important to the three races – to observe the changing colour of the leaves and the changing behaviour of the animals so they recognize the messages the land sent.

I have incorporated these three cultures, but the same could apply to most of the other older indigenous races. To my mind, as the three have survived for 60,000 odd years they have had plenty of time to observe nature and to understand spiritual law. Yet, when the colonisers arrived, they were treated with disdain, used for slaves, and plundered.

Colonisers may have known about the sciences but they did not know about spiritual law, and for me, I know which is the most important. This view reflects who was really advanced, and who was ignorant.

Perhaps it is indicative of fear, where the brutality of man was exerted over peace loving and spiritual races to the point of extermination. The Aborigines and the Native of America (both North and South America) were systematically ravaged and annihilated (many still consider it is happening today). Sadly, the same applied to The Bushman, where extermination was first carried out by other African tribes, and then the European invaders.

Their 60,000 years of occupation and observation gave them understanding of the delicate balance and relationship with all things, on and off Mother Earth – they have three principles of learning. These are; watching, seeing and hearing. All require present conscious attention and awareness as taught in this book. They all had healers whose precepts were endowed from relationship and respect. Psychic healing and psychic surgery were performed with the spirits in attendance. They listened to the lessons of nature as they knew that nature was the best teacher.

Spiritual wisdom as lived and understood by these cultures should have been a wonderful window of opportunity for Westerners, as a catalyst for mass spiritual development. But in arrogance, Western man scorned it. But perhaps there is another way, where their wisdom seeps over time to lead us to a better way – one that raises our consciousness, and one that imbues us with respect for the Earth and all creatures on it.

Apology

Not being an Australian Aborigine, Native American, or Bushman of the Kalahari cultures, I have had to imagine beyond my research to fill in the gaps of knowledge (I have worked with all three races in different ways). If my imagining has offended in some way, I apologize as I mean no disrespect, and only tried to capture the essence of spiritual connection of the three cultures. Further to this, from the website http://aiatsis.gov.au/sites/default/files/docs/asp/ethical-publishing-guidelines.pdf   I have taken the following …In the same way that there's no single Aboriginal or Torres Strait Islander identity, there's no single approach to the many challenges and opportunities of producing material by and about Aboriginal and Torres Strait Islander peoples. The same could apply to the different nations and cultures of indigenous Americans. And so, it is possible that I have offended some, but in view of the fact that the various cultures differ so much, once again I ask for their indulgence an apologies.

Connection to the land

In this book you have learnt of spirit and ego, of moving from fear to love, and throughout the book about connection to the land. But what is this connection to the land that all indigenous races have? You read the intuitive message that Stevie received from Mother *Earth, I'm dying, slowly dying, yet nobody listens, no body cares…*

Most non-indigenous people cannot understand what is not seen or felt. But it is different, very different, for the indigenous people, for they do see and feel the land. It is just as alive for them as your being able to see a tree or pickup and feel a stone. But that is where the connection for most ends. However, for the indigenous people their connection is much deeper – a seventh sense that has been developed through thousands of years of living within the fold of nature.

As a non-indigenous person I have been blessed to been able to experience an essence of that connection. My experiences are puny in relation to those of the indigenous person who grew up with the land. But nevertheless, what I have seen and felt is enough to convince me that there is much more than what we see. I shall relate some of these.

For most nonindigenous people they would consider that the spiritual connection that the indigenous people have for the landscape is mystical. It may be for non-indigenous people, but how can something, which is commonplace in the everyday life of the indigenous people be mystical – it isn't.

For everything is consciousness, the fact that most westerners cannot see it, does not mean it is not there.

And now, after having lived in the midst of an Aboriginal community for seven months, lived in Africa for over thirty years, and studied the Native American Tradition, I am even more convinced of their developed senses.

If the fulfilment and delineation of the human person with social, natural and supernatural setting is a universally valid measure for the evaluation of culture, primitive societies are our primitive superiors.

Jared Diamond

Notes on the bushmen – a vanishing race.

Not wanting to clutter the story, here I include items of interest.

So adapted to his harsh environment, the Bushman was able to store food reserves in the form of carbohydrates in the stomach and behind. This clearly indicates that for this evolution, he must have been in the Kalahari region for many thousands of years. Yet, they were obliterated by man in one short century. Now there are only a few remnants of the once spiritual race. And even now the Botswana Government has recently relocated some of the remaining few from their spiritual home so they can mine diamonds.

To the opinion of the earlier explorers, the art of the Bushman was without form. However, it is clear to see that there is specific and spiritual form, where animals and man have lines or links heading skyward, depicting a spiritual connection. The same applied to the Australian Aboriginal works, where the early explorers announced that there was no form to the work. This work also shows links from human figures to the sky. Should you want to confirm this, there are many websites you can go to.

The following is from the pen of Van der Post, which relates to the spirituality of the Bushman. He wrote …

We start off discussing a set of hills in Northern Botswana called Slippery Hills. These are or were sacred to the Bushman and a place of ritual…

…Van der Post describes his first sighting … the lift of remote hills produced immediate emotion and experienced forthwith that urge to devotion, which once made hills and mountains sacred to man, one was in the presence of an act of spirit as much as a feature of geology. The nearer we came the stronger the impression grew to communicate their own atmosphere to us.

Later, Van der Post explained that upon wanting to film some of the many sacred Bushman rock paintings, the camera did not work – the reel kept jamming. Over six different reels were tried and even though the camera had been stripped, cleaned and oiled – twice, it still would not work. Yet it worked just before the Slippery Hills visit. It also worked immediately afterwards.

The same applied to the sound recorder. It worked one minute, the next it didn't.

Apparently, these paintings have never faded, even though they have been exposed to the elements, and are hundreds of years old.

Again, Van der Post…

Another indicator of a strong spiritual connection is that the Bushman seems, on occasions, to be immune to attacks by lions. Perhaps the sacredness of life was felt by both, but there are stories of shared kills, or where a Bushman would walk through a pride of lions, instead of taking a wide circle around them as we would. The lions let them pass without incident. This is astonishing as there are two times when lions are particularly aggressive. One, is when a cub is born. The other is when they have made a kill, and are with the kill…

When the Bushman were in trance by the fire, as the story gave, Stevie pondered the word N/um that was shouted. N/um is an Ikung word that means Kundalini rising. Once awakened, the state I called trance, was what they refer to as !kia or Kundalini. They would dance for hours to raise the N/um to a state of !kia.

Once, when in a meditation I asked Weishka how he died in that life and was told, "I had become slow and old and could no longer trot like a wild dog. The day came for the clan to move on and I would have been a burden. Knowing that there is no death, this is not a time of worry. But it was one of sadness. The younger ones built a shelter of acacia thorns to protect me from the wild animals. In the shelter was placed all the food and water that they could spare.

With tears in all of our eyes, we said our goodbyes before they trotted over the hill and out of site to a route that I had been on many times.

I used that time to meditate and show gratitude for a life rich in love and fullness. But

I was also tired from a long harsh life, and so slept a lot. At one time a leopard came but the shelter held, and it finally went. With the food and water consumed, and failing strength, the hyenas finally broke in and consumed my spirit. It is good this way as many animals gave of themselves for our survival and I did the same. I felt no pain, as joy flooded my mind. Many of the old died this way. We die with courage and the oneness of all."

He also told me that many people say that they hope that they will 'pass over' in their sleep. No, hope that it happens with your full consciousness, as it is a glorious time – just imagine.

∞

The following poem was sent to me by friend and writing mentor, Dorian Haarhoff, after he had read and advised on the manuscript:

What if you slept?
And what if, in your sleep, you dreamed?
And what if, in your dream, you went to Heaven
and there plucked a rare and beautiful flower?
And what if, when you awoke, you had the flower in your hand?
Ah, what then?

--- Samuel Taylor Coleridge (1772-1834)

B I B L I O G R A P H Y

The Projection of the Astral Body by Sylvan Muldoon & Hereward Carrington 0-87728-062-x Weiser Books

Voices of our Ancestors Dhyani Ywahoo Shambhala

The Lost World of the Kalahari, by Lourens Van der Post.

Love Equals Power, by Eileen McBride

Spiritual Nutrition, by Gabriel Coussens MD. ISBN 9781556434990

My Dreaming People, by Max Dulumunmun Harrison Finch Publishing

http://www.creativespirits.info/aboriginalculture/history/aboriginal-history-timeline.html

http://www.lasseteria.com/CYCLOPEDIA/215.htm

Walkabout refers to a spiritual rite of passage that a young Aboriginal will undertake

http://www.grandpapencil.net/austral/abword/abm.htm

http://www.dingo.livingin-australia.com/dingo-facts.html

KATS – Journal of Transpersonal Psychology

http://en.wikipedia.org/wiki/Renal_failure

voices of the first day, Awakening in the aboriginal dreamtime. By Robert Lawlor

The Power of Myth – Joseph Campbell

Pilke's Book of Hours, love Poems to God – Rainer Maria Rilke

PAT GRAYSON HAS WRITTEN THE FOLLOWING BOOKS:

Seeds of Potentiality, an anthology of positivity

Oh Hell

How to write – Right!

Trees, the guardians of the soul

"The Intelligence", a state of equanimity.

Yogi, the tails and teaching of a suburban alpha doggie

Know ThySelf (volumes one and two)

Chinese Down Under

Gruffian's bare teddy bear (a children's storybook)

Life, does it have to be fair (a young adults books of positive stories)

Pat has also collaborated on other writings, and worked on over forty books for his writing clients.

To contact Pat Grayson for workshops, speaking engagements

pat@heartspacepublications.com

www.heartspacepublications.com